The Hou

An Outer Banks Mystery

By Jayne Conrad Harding

Sequel to *Out of the Mist: An Outer Banks Mystery*

For Lee.

And for the endangered, wild horses that still live along the Corolla shores.

The Song of Wandering Aengus

by William Butler Yeats

I went out to the hazel wood,
Because a fire was in my head,
And cut and peeled a hazel wand,
And hooked a berry to a thread;
And when white moths were on the wing,
And moth-like stars were flickering out,
I dropped the berry in a stream
And caught a little silver trout.

When I had laid it on the floor
I went to blow the fire a-flame,
But something rustled on the floor,
And someone called me by my name:
It had become a glimmering girl
With apple blossom in her hair
Who called me by my name and ran
And faded through the brightening air.

Though I am old with wandering
Through hollow lands and hilly lands,
I will find out where she has gone,
And kiss her lips and take her hands;
And walk among long dappled grass,
And pluck till time and times are done,
The silver apples of the moon,
The golden apples of the sun.

Chapter 1

A blustery, spring wind caught hold of the screen door of The Old Village Store in Corolla, North Carolina. But Zoe Hamilton managed to open it and, with difficulty, kept it from slamming back into the outside wall.

In fact, she caught it just in time and closed it tightly before pushing her way into the store.

As usual, the smell of strong, freshly-brewed coffee permeated the air. But Rose Hoskins, the owner, was neither behind the counter nor seated in her comfortable arm-chair, nearby.

In spite of the roaring wind outside the store, the sky was a brilliant blue, the air was clear, and the sunshine created razor-sharp shadows from all objects in its path.

It was a beautiful day. Zoe had only lived in the Outer Banks for six months, but knew early on that it was "home." She liked the freedom of working as a consultant instead of as a full-time museum curator, which she had done for 14 years.

She had enough money to live independently for the time being, though the cost of her independence had been high. Her husband died in Iraq, leaving her alone with their 12-year-old daughter, Kate, their German shepherd, Woolf, and a substantial insurance policy.

Since his death and her subsequent move to the Outer Banks, she had adopted another daughter, Sarah, who was only a few months younger than Kate.

Zoe glanced around as she unwound her blue, woolly scarf, and finally spotted Rose standing in a far corner of the large, one-roomed store. She was talking with her childhood friend, Susan Hall.

Rose was a tall, easy-going woman whose typical expression included an easy smile. At the moment though, given the serious frowns on both their faces, and the fact that they were sequestered in the back of the room, they obviously did not want to be interrupted.

And, since neither of them was particularly secretive by nature, and in fact, they were more inclined to gossip, their isolation in the back of the store was somewhat troubling.

Their gossip was not the unkind sort. Instead, they indulged in more "newsy" types of gossip that included incidents such as who was in the hospital, who had recently sold their home and moved, and so on.

Fortunately for Zoe, both Rose and Susan had, early on, welcomed her as a friend. In fact, most people in the Outer Banks had welcomed her, much to her relief. Her greatest concern was not to be an outsider in the small, tight-knit community. But fortunately, that hadn't happened.

Zoe did not interrupt the two women. Instead, she pulled out one of the wire baskets near the counter and began to gather the few things she had come in to buy.

In addition to the necessities, Rose managed to stock some more unusual things as well, including the brand of Belgian chocolate that Zoe liked to use when she baked.

The store, itself, could only be described as cozy. A few strategically-placed chairs offered spouses and tired children places to rest so that shoppers didn't feel as rushed as they might have done.

An electric kettle with fresh water stood on a table for those who wanted tea or cocoa, and an electric coffee pot was always plugged in, as well. Usually, an open box of cookies or a container of Virginia peanuts sat nearby.

Cheery, red-checked curtains allowed ample sunlight into the room where shelves were clean and items were neatly arranged.

It was quiet; no one else was in the store, though plenty of early shoppers often dropped in to pick up coffee or something for their lunches on their way to work. Sometimes, they just came in to have a quick cup of coffee and to see Rose.

By the time Zoe had leisurely finished her shopping and had set her basket up on the counter, Rose called to her from the back of the room.

"Hey, Zoe, we were so deep in talk that I didn't even hear you come in. Then again, maybe I'm just going deaf."

She grinned as she scurried back up the aisle and slid behind the counter. She wore a bright-red sweater and matching earrings, and a large, silver charm bracelet that tinkled as she rang up groceries.

"I'm telling you, Honey, old age ain't for sissies."

Zoe laughed. "I wouldn't put you in that category just yet, Rose. You're one of the most energetic people I know. More than I am, as a matter of fact."

As they chatted, Susan also wandered back to the front of the store and leaned against the end of the counter while Zoe pulled out her wallet. She was normally so talkative that Zoe wondered at her silence.

"How are you, Susan?" she asked. "I've tried to call you a few times lately, but haven't been able to catch up with you. I figured that you must be busy."

7

When Zoe had first rented a house in Corolla the previous autumn, Susan had impressed her as being the last person on earth with whom she wanted to become acquainted.

As it turned out though, she had judged the older woman too hastily and had subsequently been ashamed of herself for it.

Susan was neither the scattered, nor somewhat scary, person that she sometimes appeared to be. And in the end, it was Susan who was partially responsible for the fact that Zoe, Kate, and Sarah, were still alive.

The remainder of the credit for that was due to a local deputy, Hugh McKenzie, though it was chiefly due to a Ghost Horse that had literally leapt out of a local legend and had come to their aid at the last, crucial moment.

Susan's expression was cautious as she met Zoe's eyes. "I'm sorry, Honey. I've been a little preoccupied. In fact," she glanced around as though checking to see if anyone else was listening, "I need to pick up a few things here myself, and now I can't even remember what they were."

A slight tremor came into her voice. "You see, my mother passed away recently."

Zoe touched the older woman's arm. "I really am sorry, Susan. I had no idea." She glanced at Rose who was, at that moment, focusing on something outside the window. "What can I do to help?"

"Oh, nothing really," she answered. "Actually, my mother had been living down in Florida for a few years, so there probably aren't many folks around here who even remember her. It's just hard, though. I know you understand."

Zoe lifted a bag of groceries. "I sure do. We never quite get over those kinds of losses, do we?"

While her mother's death could explain Susan's quietness, it did not explain why the two women had been so secretive. But Susan didn't say any more, and an awkward silence fell between them.

Zoe scooped up her other bag, determined to mind her own business. "I need to get going. Take care of yourself, and let me know if you need anything." Just as she reached the door, Susan called to her.

"Actually Zoe…there might be something you can help me with, if you want." Rose's eyebrows shot up in surprise and she stared at Susan, who guiltily met her questioning look.

"Well," her voice sounded defensive, "maybe she *can* help me. And besides, I think we can trust her. Don't you?"

Rose came out from behind the counter and put an arm around Zoe's shoulders.

"You took me by surprise, Susie, that's all. And, if you really want my opinion, I think you're wise to include Zoe. I trust her, too." Having said that, she slipped back behind the counter to retrieve her coffee cup.

"The thing is," Rose took a sip of her now-cold coffee, "It's not my place to offer you advice unless I'm asked. But honestly, this is too much for just the two of us to sort out."

Susan nodded and sank down into the old armchair next to the counter. She looked pale and exhausted, and older than Zoe had seen her look before.

"Come on, Rose, I have been asking for your advice for the last two days," she snapped. Her mouth was a firm, tight line.

9

"Because I don't know what to do. So don't act like I haven't given you permission to give me advice."

Rose rolled her eyes and gathered her patience. "I *mean* that you don't need my permission to ask Zoe for help. Or anyone else that you want to ask, for that matter."

"Do what feels best to you, and talk to whomever you want."

Susan's lips grew thinner and Zoe, who did not want to be involved in an argument between the two of them, decided that it was time to leave.

"Well, I'm around whenever you feel like talking. Call or come by whenever you want," she said.

She sat the bags back down on the counter long enough to button her coat and retie her scarf. "And," she added, "I'll do anything I can to help you. You know that."

Impulsively, Susan asked, "Do you have time to come with me to *The Silver Shores Tea Room*, right now?"

Zoe frowned. "Sure. The only thing I really need to do today is pick up the girls from school at 3:00. But otherwise, I'm free."

"Great." Susan managed a thin smile as she stood up and smoothed the front of her denim skirt. "I'm ready whenever you are." She glanced at Rose, who looked relieved and nodded her encouragement.

"You ladies go drink tea and mull things over," she said. "I have no doubt that Zoe will help you figure things out, Susan. Anyway, three heads are better than two, I always say."

"Though I suppose it depends whose heads we're talking about." She chuckled at her own joke. "In this case, it's a good third head."

When *The Silver Shores Tea Room* had opened four months earlier, everyone speculated about Jean Burich's chances for success. But Jean also served good coffee and lemonade, along with a nice selection of small sandwiches, baked goods, and ice cream. And her freshly-baked scones were legendary.

Jean's daughter, Hanna, greeted them with a friendly smile and led them to a table in a corner next to a sunny window.

Zoe ordered a large pot of tea and an assortment of sandwiches. They chatted about the weather and their spring bulbs, as well as what Zoe's daughters were up to, until Hanna emerged with the tea and sandwiches, and carefully arranged the trays, plates, and cups on the table.

Susan seemed to be a little more relaxed and Zoe watched her heap an impressive amount of sugar into her cup, take a few careful sips, and then add even more. She involuntarily shuddered, but fortunately, Susan didn't appear to notice.

"Thanks for coming here with me," she said. "I have no doubt that I am complicating everything more than it needs to be. I've always been good at that."

Zoe gave her an encouraging smile. "I certainly hope that's true in this case."

Susan took a small bite of an egg-salad sandwich. "You already know about my mother's recent death. The trouble is that I've inherited the house she owned here."

"Actually, it was 'home' to my family for nearly 170 years, but I moved out as soon as I could."

Zoe frowned. "So she still owned the house here, but she spent all her time in Florida?"

"Yes." Susan finished her sandwich. "As I said, it's an old house. In fact, the original part predates the Civil War. But that part was morphed into a kitchen, a pantry, and a small bathroom as the house was gradually enlarged over the years."

"My family built it and kept improving it until it became a two-storied house with six bedrooms and an attic that I haven't seen the inside of for more years than I can remember. Not that I want to," she shuddered.

"It sounds like quite a grand place. Have I seen it, before? The only older houses that I am aware of aren't too far from Rose's store in Corolla. Or, is it located somewhere else on the Outer Banks?"

Susan shook her head. "No, it's actually not far from where we are right now. But you wouldn't have seen it because it sits a good-way back from the main road and in a grove of trees. It backs up to Currituck Sound and includes five-acres of land."

"Wow," Zoe said; she was impressed. "So what's the problem? It sounds lovely." She reached for the teapot and refilled both of their blue-flowered, china cups.

"I don't want to live there," Susan said, and suddenly hunched her shoulders. "But I don't want to sell it, either. The solution would be to have enough money to maintain it and keep it."

"But with a limited income, I can't possibly borrow the money and go into debt. I need to do something soon, though. There are repairs and things…" she vaguely explained.

"It's a long, complicated story and you probably don't need to know most of it. But the problem is that I can't live there and I can't sell it."

And I need money for repairs. So if you have any ideas at all, I'd be very grateful." Susan was obviously working herself back into an agitated state, but Zoe persisted because she wanted to understand the situation better.

"So, you're saying that your mother did not keep up with repairs, even though she still owned the house?"

"She kept up with some of it, but living so far away, I think it must have just slipped her mind after a while. Or maybe it just became less important to her. There is less money in her estate than I'd hoped there would be."

Zoe thoughtfully stirred her tea. "Well, if you decide to sell, you'll have realtors, and probably developers too, lining up to talk to you."

"That kind of a property has to be worth a lot of money. Especially with five acres of land along the Sound."

"Meanwhile," she added, "I would be happy to come and look around. Maybe if I actually see it I'll be able to think of a good way to help you."

"You could consider renting it, you know," she added. "Once you make repairs, that is."

Relief flooded Susan's face. She heaped more sugar into her refilled cup and reached for one, last sandwich. "It really does need some work," she repeated.

"I'm not sure that I want to rent it out, but I do want to show it to you. Can you come now? As soon as we're finished, here?"

Chapter 2

The wind was even stronger by the time Zoe carefully followed Susan's car onto a gravel-and-weed-covered lane that was half hidden between two overgrown holly bushes.

No wonder she had never noticed this place. Unless someone already knew about it, they would have no idea that it existed.

The two cars slowly passed swaying, old trees and overgrown areas that had once been gardens, until they finally stopped in front of a white, clapboard house sheltered within a grove of trees.

Dark green shutters bordered the front windows on three floors, and a wide porch with plenty of room for comfortable chairs led to the worn-looking, front door.

The place undoubtedly needed some work, but it would be quite nice if restored. Zoe wondered why Susan didn't want to live here. It was private, and the gardens could either be restored or transformed into grass. It was, quite simply, a charming house in a beautiful setting.

If Susan sold her own house, there would be enough money to restore a significant portion, if not all, of this one. Then again, she wouldn't be living on the ocean if she moved here.

The surrounding trees were mostly pin-oaks with marvelously-shaped branches. Pine trees were also scattered throughout the grounds, interspersed with a few, large magnolias.

Early clusters of daffodils randomly bloomed in the grass. Zoe got out of her Jeep and looked around. Another old house sat at a distance, across a field and to the left of Susan's.

Currituck Sound lay behind both, and Zoe's attention was soon drawn to where the white-capped waves churned in the fierce, spring wind.

A pair of gulls swooped over the water where they fished. Zoe turned to Susan who stood quietly at her side.

"Who is your neighbor over there?" she nodded at the other house.

Susan shaded her eyes with her hand.

"Noah Brent. His family has owned that place for years."

"They were friendly with us when we were kids, but then there was some kind of disagreement. I don't know what it was about. Everything is good between us now though," she quickly added.

"We've recently become reacquainted. But we always did like each other and it's nice to be on speaking terms with him, again."

"That is good," Zoe agreed "Hopefully, he will help keep an eye on your house while it's unoccupied."

Susan nodded. "He does." She turned and led the way up the wide, front steps and unlocked the door which was swollen from age and the recent dampness.

She shoved it hard and they went inside. Zoe waited while she wrestled the door closed again and then waved her arm.

"Well, here it is." Their footsteps clattered across the bare, heart-pine floor. Four doors opened into large rooms, two on each side of the central hall. Beyond was a wall with recessed doors on either side that led to back rooms.

Even from a distance, Zoe could see that some of the furniture was good and probably restorable, if need be. There were also some good antiques.

One example was a large, crystal chandelier that hung low over their heads and was much too large for the hallway.

Zoe thought that it might be lead crystal, and perhaps dated from the early nineteenth century. If so, it could be worth a lot of money.

Susan led her into the first room on the left, which was the living room. But then she stopped and frowned.

Finally, Zoe asked, "Would you like to show me the other rooms? Or, would you rather have me wander on my own?"

Susan jumped as though she'd been startled out of a dream. "Oh, I'll show you the rest of the house, but let's sit down here a minute, if you don't mind."

She brushed a light coating of dust from the seat of a chair while Zoe dusted the seat of another, and they both sat down.

"You know," Zoe leaned back, "This is a beautiful house and I can't imagine why you don't want to live here."

"Susan," she cleared her throat, "I have to ask. Is something wrong with either the house or this property?"

Susan slowly exhaled. "No—there's nothing wrong with it. Well…" she hesitated, "at least, not in the way that you're thinking."

Zoe's green eyes narrowed while Susan carefully examined her hands. "You see, the house is haunted."

Susan's interest in the supernatural was a major reason that Zoe had avoided her when they had first met.

There was a lot more to her than first met the eye though, and Zoe learned from her own hard experience that miracles, sometimes even supernatural ones, do happen.

She frowned. "I can't imagine that having a ghost around would bother you in the least."

"Aren't you the one who keeps track of all the local ghost legends and lore around here? I thought…"

Susan interrupted her. "Not everything," she said with an air of dignity as she zipped up the front of her jacket.

The house was downright cold and Zoe wished that she'd worn heavier socks. She was beginning to shiver. It felt much colder in the house than it was outside, and she wondered if the furnace worked.

"Is that why you don't want to sell?" Zoe asked. "Because you would have to disclose that the house is haunted?"

Susan clamped her mouth shut, but Zoe persisted in what she meant to be a gentle voice.

"If there are any ghosts here, wouldn't they just be members of your own family? You're surely not afraid of your own ancestors, are you? I mean, since you don't seem to be bothered by ghosts, in general."

"It's a tad more complicated than that," Susan stiffly replied. "There's a lot that you don't know, Zoe. It's not a normal situation, at all."

Zoe's patience was beginning to weaken. She was freezing, and instead of looking at the house, they were sitting in a dusty living room having a pointless conversation.

She had endured enough mysterious drama for one day and resolved to draw Susan's attention back to the immediate problem of the house. As far as metaphysical problems were concerned, Susan would have to deal with those on her own.

"I doubt that the presence of ghosts would be considered 'normal' in any situation," Zoe said.

"For now though, we have to consider the repairs that need to be done. By the way, does the central heating work?"

"It does," Susan said, relieved that Zoe was no longer talking about ghosts.

"I'm not sure that it's working well anymore, though. And the plumbing and electrical wiring are old and should be replaced."

"It needs a new roof, too," she added. "There is some water damage in a couple of the upstairs rooms."

"Okay, then we'll need estimates to find out what all of that will cost, and you'll need to fill me in on which are the best companies to work with."

"Noah will help with that," Susan waved a dismissive hand. "He used to work as a contractor and seems to know everybody around here better than I do."

"Wonderful." Zoe nodded her approval. That will speed things up. How soon can you talk to him?"

"Anytime," Susan answered. "He's retired now, and his two kids are grown and gone, so it's just he and his wife living over there."

"Her name is Analee and she's not as friendly as he is, but Noah told me that she suffers from some sort of nervous condition, and she's generally uncomfortable around other people."

"Growing up here in this house was not easy, I can tell you," she went on. "Living in a nice house isn't what matters, you know. It's love, isn't it. And a sense of comfort, and of family, and of belonging."

"Yes, it is," Zoe agreed in surprise.

Susan continued. "In the end, all that really matters is whether you loved and were loved in return."

She heaved a resigned sigh and headed for the door. "Come along, and I'll show you the house. Then you'll see for yourself what needs to be done."

The two women methodically looked into each room on the ground floor while Susan told Zoe as much as she knew about the furnishings and what, as far as she knew, needed to be repaired. Zoe took notes.

Then they circled back and climbed the wide, pine stairs to the second floor where the cold was even more intense. Oddly so, it seemed to Zoe. After all, warmth was supposed to rise, wasn't it?

The upper landing was dark, as was the upstairs hallway. Dark brown paneling lined the walls and deadened the already-dim light that shone from the four ceiling fixtures.

The doors to each of the six bedrooms were open. But the light from their windows did not penetrate the darkness, at all.

Zoe felt oddly uneasy as they progressed from room to room. She knew that all houses have a particular feel. In fact, she had worked in some house-museums that were not welcoming places. But if there were ghosts in those houses, they had not interfered with her work, nor had they made her feel this uneasy. Not to the extent that this house did, anyway.

Whether there were actually ghosts in the house or not, the air was certainly heavy, even thick, with the past. And it was an uncomfortable past, at that.

At the end of the hall a plain, narrow staircase led to the third floor. Zoe pointed at it. "Are we going to the attic, too?"

Susan visibly shuddered and said, "No. That attic is stuffed with who-knows-what and I'm not up to looking at it, today. We'll do it another time, but not until we have to."

That was fine with Zoe, who could hardly stop herself from rushing back down the stairs. Susan reached out and took ahold of her arm just as they reached the bedroom near the landing.

"I know we've already looked in here, but I want you to know that this was my room when I was a child. It was painted bright-yellow then." A faint smile grew as she lightly touched one of the walls.

"My parents thought it should be papered and trimmed in light pink or lavender, but I held out for bright-yellow paint and white trim."

Zoe, who was finding comfort in the close proximity of the stairway, smiled. "So, you were an individual with your own strong opinions, even then."

Susan looked pleased. "Back then, I was much more certain about what I wanted, and I also thought I knew all the answers. Except to this house."

She absently stroked the faded, yellow wall. "Let's go downstairs," she suddenly said. "I don't like being up here.

Truthfully, neither of them wanted to stay in the house any longer, and they quickly gathered up their things.

Once they were out in the sunshine again, Susan turned the key in the lock and asked, "Do you believe that old saying, that the "sins of the fathers" are "visited" on their children?"

Her question surprised Zoe. But instead of rushing down the front steps as she'd intended, she stopped and absentmindedly scraped at one of the faded, white railings with her fingernail.

21

"That's quite a question, Susan."

The older woman nodded and looked away. "Yes, I know it is."

"What I believe," Zoe finally said, "is that it depends on whether or not the children have knowingly kept committing the "sins" of their fathers, or not."

"I mean, if parents purposely do something terrible and their children knowingly do the same, then that's one thing. But if the children are not like their parents, and they don't want to do terrible things, then that's something else, again."

"You think then, that if the children or descendants of a family are innocent, they won't be punished for the actions of their ancestors?" Susan bit her lower lip and her hand remained on the door-knob.

New life, new color, new growth flourished all around them. Could there be anything less for human beings, as well? There was always death, but there was always life, too.

Zoe looked at the new, green leaf-buds on the oak trees nearby and said, "Yes—that is exactly what I mean."

The older woman sighed and turned away from the door. Zoe went to her and put an arm around her shoulder.

"You don't have to tell me why you asked that, Susan. What I do know, is that you are a very good person and I don't believe for one moment that you will be visited by the "sins" of your fathers, whatever they might have been."

Susan blinked away unexpected tears. "Thank you, my dear. That was a lovely thing to say to a scared, old woman."

She sniffed. "And now, if you can think of any legal way to raise money to fix this place up, let me know."

"I certainly will," Zoe agreed. "Meanwhile, why don't you come home with me? I am planning to stitch up some curtains for the kitchen, and could use your help. I'm not much of a seamstress, but I saw some fabric that I fell in love with."

Susan reached into her bag for a tissue. "That sounds like fun."

"We'll have more tea or some coffee if you'd like. And you can come with me to pick up the girls, later."

"Let's stop by *The Cotton Gin*, on the way home, too. They have a gorgeous, framed print of the wild horses that I want, and I'll pick up a bottle of wine for dinner."

Zoe and Susan both lived along a remote stretch of the Corolla beach where there were no roads. Once they reached the end of the paved street, or as Kate liked to say, "The border to the Otherworld," they needed 4-wheel drive in order to continue the rest of the way.

They drove down a sand dune and turned left where a wide stretch of sand extended as far as the eye could see.

Dunes sprinkled with sea oats and tough grasses rose to their left, where some small groups of houses were scattered.

To their right lay the Atlantic Ocean. The waves were rough and the white caps reflected sunlight and shades of deep blue and green.

Chapter 3

Later that afternoon, Kate and Sarah sat at the kitchen table eating blueberry yogurt and potato chips.

"I'm glad to see that you're both really conscientious about eating right," she teased as she removed clothes from the dryer, within sight of the girls.

Their German shepherd, Woolf, lay at Kate's feet, not exactly begging but with a pleading look in his eyes.

She looked directly at her mother as she dropped a chip and he snapped it up. Zoe wagged her finger and laughed. "Not too many of those, Kate."

Kate rolled her eyes in response, but couldn't stop herself from grinning.

"Come on, Mom, he needs a snack, too. And, we're not so very bad, are we Sarah?" She gently poked the arm of the quiet, dark-haired girl sitting next to her.

Sarah pulled another handful of chips out of the bag. "I remember reading that everyone needs some fat and salt in their diets and I'm just trying to make sure that I have enough, every day."

Zoe laughed. As the girls chatted, she closely watched Sarah, relieved to see that her adopted daughter was doing so well.

Before coming to live with them, Sarah had only known a difficult life with no mother, and a step-father who didn't care for her.

To crown it all, her step-father had attempted to kill her, along with Zoe and Kate, because Zoe had discovered that he was a smuggler who illegally imported artifacts from the Middle East, to sell.

But he was dead now. And the memory of him needed to die as well.

"Mom," Kate looked thoughtfully at her mother. "Is Ms. Susan okay? She seemed kind of quiet, today."

She wound a strand of hair around one finger and observed, "That's not like her, at all."

She scooped out the last of her yogurt, got up, and threw the container in the trash.

"Ms. Susan is worried about keeping a house that her mother owned near Corolla, but she doesn't want to sell it, either," Zoe explained. Kate opened her mouth but her mother interrupted her.

"I'm not sure why, Kate." Zoe pushed back her red-gold hair. "She doesn't seem to want to talk about it.

"But," she added, "I'm going to try to help her come up with a solution to at least get some repairs made to the place."

"Meanwhile, you girls think about it, too. Sometimes you come up with better ideas than I do. And besides, she needs help from all of her friends, not just from me."

She tucked the clothes basket under one arm. "I need to get back to fixing dinner."

"I am laying your clothes on your beds, girls, so you put them away as soon as you come upstairs. Do you two have homework?"

"We do, Mom," Kate admitted, "but first, I want to be outside in the sunlight for a while. Being cooped up in classrooms all day makes me feel like I can't breathe." She slid her chair back and stood up.

"Want to come with me, Sarah?"

As usual, Sarah did. She seemed to generally follow Kate's lead and Zoe hoped that, with time, she would become more assertive.

26

Meanwhile though, she was secure and loved, and there was a lot to be said for that.

Her thoughts wandered back to what Susan had said that morning about the "sins of the fathers" and her belief that love was more important than anything else, and she wondered what was really bothering Susan.

Kate loved the sea and never tired of walking along the shore and hunting for shells, though heaven knew that she had accumulated enough of them to fill every drawer in her dresser, and then some.

And though she never admitted it to Sarah or anyone else, she also liked to go every day to visit the place where she had last seen the Ghost Horse, the previous fall.

He had appeared to her one last time, the night that she and her mother, and Sarah, had nearly died.

He had stood in the water, waiting for her to come. When she waded into the summer-warmed sea (Kate shivered at the memory), she had also seen a shadowy figure standing beside the horse, resting a hand on the white stallion's proud neck. She had waded toward him, trying to reach him.

When the scudding clouds passed over the moon so that she could see more clearly, she had realized with a shock, that the figure standing next to the horse was her own father.

She believed it was proof that he was still with them and was protecting them, as best he could.

Kate didn't really expect to see either the horse or her father again on these daily trips, but just being in that place by the shore made her feel closer to both of them.

Chapter 4

Susan was much more cheerful by the time she went home, and she admitted to herself that she was even feeling a little excited.

She had telephoned Noah from Zoe's house earlier in the afternoon, and he recommended a couple of good roofing companies to contact.

One man had already agreed to come around the following day, and she took that as a good sign. Maybe she really was complicating her problems more than they needed to be.

She ate an early dinner and then moved some smaller pieces of furniture so that she could add some of her mother's things from the old house.

She didn't need or want much of it, and was surprised to have found herself feeling sentimental and unable to let go of everything. She hadn't expected that.

Since her mother's death, Susan had been nearly paralyzed with indecision. She still wasn't sure what to do, but taking one step at a time might help her realistically face all of her options along the way.

Long before that could happen though, she needed to sort through the huge accumulation of things that her family had acquired over the years. She dreaded it, but maybe some of the items were valuable, or at least saleable, and would help pay for the repairs.

Surely some of it had value. After all, her family was wealthy for a number of years. Granted, some of her ancestors might also have been insane, but at least they were well-off.

"There's no time like the present," she told herself. As much as she dreaded getting started, it had to be done. Once she got into it, maybe she would feel less overwhelmed.

The evening shadows would soon be deepening over Corolla, and she didn't want to be in the house alone after dark. But the thought of doing something constructive cheered her up and gave her some unexpected courage.

"I have been much too afraid," she told herself, "and I am tired of being afraid. It really does wear one out."

The sense of optimism and courage stayed with her until she turned onto the darkening, gravel lane that led to the house, and then she suddenly began to lose her nerve.

Was it wise to have come, alone? But the lights shining from Noah Brent's windows across the field were comforting. At least someone was reasonably nearby, and she could speed-dial him from her phone, if need be.

Once Susan turned the key in the lock and shifted the stubborn, swollen door, fear unaccountably rose over her like the ice-cold tide of a winter sea.

Maybe she should just leave and come the next day. But since she was already here, and was well-armed with her cell-phone and pepper spray, she decided to stay.

Could one actually pepper-spray a ghost? She wondered as she went into the living room and laid her things down.

Everything seems worse at night, she reminded herself. Corolla was such a small community that everyone knew everyone else, and she reasonably could not think that anyone meant her any harm.

So, what was she afraid of? The house, itself? Being alone in the dark? She sighed at her own foolishness.

However, that didn't keep her from glancing over her shoulder one last time before firmly locking the door and shutting out the night.

She turned on a couple of lamps that sat on small tables on either side of the hallway entrance, and decided to tackle the living room first. It was closest to the outside door in case she wanted to leave in a hurry.

Susan glanced at the old-fashioned, black telephone and was reminded that she needed to have the service cut-off as soon as possible. She would do that first-thing in the morning, and then set up a time for Zoe to come back to look over the furniture and paintings.

She took off her coat and threw it over the arm of the red, brocade couch and looked around. She would begin by emptying the small, end-table drawers which took a lot longer than expected.

It was amazing just how much paper and assorted odds and ends could be successfully crammed into small, tight places.

Fortunately, she had remembered to pack a box of trash bags in with the cleaning supplies, because nearly everything, so far, was worthless.

Nearly an hour and a half later, Susan had filled two trash bags. She considered calling it a night, but changed her mind and decided to examine the contents of an old, walnut chest-on-frame, instead.

The rich, dark wood was beautiful, and she gently took hold of one of the brass drawer-pulls and looked at it. Maybe she would keep this piece.

The top drawers were not reachable, so she started with the bottom ones and worked her way up.

Finally, she went to the kitchen and brought back a wooden chair to reach the top drawer.

She carefully climbed onto it and pulled it open. When she was about half-way through with the sorting, she threw a handful of papers onto the floor and abruptly stopped. She'd heard the sound of a creaking door.

At first, she wondered if one of the windows was open. But she had checked them that morning when she'd brought Zoe over. Maybe she had missed one of them.

Susan knew that she would have to recheck the windows even as she fought the urge to grab her things and run for the car.

In the end, she summoned up her failing courage and vainly attempted to tiptoe across the creaking floor and up the stairs.

After what seemed like an eternity, she reached the landing and switched on the dim, overhead lights, thankful that the electricity had not yet been turned off.

All was quiet. Maybe a small animal or a bird had come in through one of the two chimneys that were positioned on either side of the house.

She crept down the hall, flipping on the light switches in each room along the way. All of the windows were closed and locked, just as she had thought.

Unbidden childhood memories and fears grew larger in her mind until she could hardly stop herself from running back down the stairs and out the front door.

Instead, she scurried back down and returned to the relative safety of the living room.

Maybe the family ghosts were responsible for the sounds she'd heard.   At least so far, nothing had either chased or attacked her.

She glanced at her watch and saw that it wasn't that late. She would finish sorting that one, last drawer, and then she would go home.

Chapter 5

The front door opened just as Zoe was setting the table for dinner and she recognized Hugh McKenzie's footsteps before she saw him. They met each other the previous fall when Zoe rented a house in Corolla for a few weeks.

It was the subsequent drama that nearly resulted in her death, as well as the deaths of her daughters, that had really forced them to examine their feelings for each other, and they had been dating ever since.

"Hello, Sweetheart," he called as he came into the room and dropped his keys on the counter.

"You really shouldn't leave that door unlocked, even when you're expecting me. Is everything okay? How's my best girl?"

He pulled her to himself in a quick, tight embrace. He said pretty much the same thing every evening when he came by after work, but she found that comforting. And he had shown himself to be sincerely interested in their small, everyday affairs.

Zoe genuinely loved her first husband, David. He had been quiet and introspective, whereas Hugh figuratively wore his heart on his sleeve at all times.

In a way, that made things easier because one always knew what Hugh thought and felt at any given moment, though admittedly, there were times when a little more reserve on his part might have better served his interests.

Zoe was also introspective, and closely guarded her thoughts and words. Perhaps too much, she reflected.

Hugh mildly complained that he was sometimes unable to 'read' her. He argued that any good relationship should include an openness in which both parties could sense the moods and thoughts of the other.

Hugh was also gently pushing her to marry him, but she wasn't ready. They had only known each other for a few months, and she wanted to be completely sure, no matter how long that took.

Zoe had first rented a house on the Corolla shore while she was finishing a collections book for a museum in Virginia where she worked at the time. However, she had encountered much more than she'd bargained for.

Once everything was happily sorted out though, at least for herself and the girls, she had quit her job and moved to Corolla.

She was fortunate to have found another rental house in the same area, along the unpaved shores where the wild horses lived.

A small herd of them, descendants of the original Spanish mustangs that had first swum ashore 500 years earlier, could be seen fairly often. They were usually on the dunes or at the ocean's edge, but sometimes they came close to the houses, as well.

Zoe, and her friends and family, knew better than to either approach the horses or attempt to feed them. After all, they were wild.

Sometimes, well-meaning people offered the horses food, which generally made them sick and sometimes even resulted in their deaths.

Legally, no one is allowed to come within 50 feet of the horses. While Zoe and the girls respected and obeyed that law, they did love seeing them.

In fact, Kate had recently asked if she could work as a volunteer at the Wild Horse Fund in Corolla. Zoe hadn't given her an answer yet, but was planning to say "yes."

She answered Hugh's question. "It's all fine. Nothing too awfully exciting happened today."

"Okay, then pressing on to a more important question," he teased, "What's for dinner?"

She leaned against him for a moment and he kissed her, again. Then he took off his jacket, carefully folded it, and laid it across the arm of a chair in the darkened living room.

Zoe pushed her hair back behind one ear. "One of these evenings, I'm going to say 'nothing at all,' when you ask, and then what will you do?"

"Then," he grinned, "I will bundle you and the girls into the car and take you out to eat."

"Is that what I have to do to get to go out to eat? Thank you—I'll keep that in mind," she joked.

Zoe reached into the oven and pulled out a large, covered dish filled with roast beef and vegetables, and set it on the counter. She reached for a platter and then a bowl for the gravy she would make, and readdressed his first question.

"Actually, something important did happen today, Hugh. Something is up with Susan, and Rose undoubtedly knows what it is, but neither of them wants to explain it to me.

"The only bit I know," she added, "is that Susan's mother recently died. She has asked me to help her think of some way to raise money so that she can keep her mother's house."

Hugh looked puzzled. "Why wouldn't she either just sell her own house or sell her mother's? Unless she's planning to rent it? That might be a good idea, actually--a good income for her, you know."

"But," he added, "what makes her think that you can help her raise money?"

"Well, I'm more than just a pretty face, you know," her green eyes narrowed. "I have worked with funding for projects in the past, just not for the benefit of a private person."

She arranged the dishes in the center of the table.

"Honestly, she continued, "I have no idea how to help her. But, there is definitely more to this situation, and I wish she would just be honest with me."

Hugh pulled out the napkins and carefully laid them to the left of each plate.

"You'll just have to let her tell you in her own way and time," he shrugged.

"But Hugh," she said, "Susan asked me if I believe that the "sins of the fathers" result in punishment for their children."

"She was talking about her own family and that sounds pretty serious, don't you think? I'm worried about her, to tell you the truth."

Just then, the back door slammed and the girls rushed into the kitchen.

"Sorry Mom!" Kate called. We lost track of the time. Anything you want us to do?"

"No. It's all ready and on the table, as you can see. Just wash your hands and come join us."

"Mom," Sarah pulled out her chair, "would it be alright if I took an art class? If not, that's okay," she quickly added. "But, I'd like to." She laid a book on the table.

"Is that a library book?" Zoe asked. "It looks like quite an old one."

Sarah nodded. "I checked it out today. We're studying mythology in our English class right now, so I went to look for another book about it and came across this one."

"It was published in 1895 or something like that. Anyway, what is really cool about it, are the illustrations of the gods and goddesses. I'm going to copy the ones that I think are especially beautiful.

Zoe placed her hand on the girl's shoulder. "I think that is a marvelous idea, Sarah, and so is the art class. Who is teaching it, and where will it be held?

Just in time, she stopped herself from also asking the cost. This was the first time that Sarah had asked her for anything, and Zoe found herself holding her breath in case Sarah suddenly changed her mind.

Zoe was always concerned that the girl might not think of herself as a true member of the family.

Her adoption had been expedited, thanks to Hugh's intervention as well as that of other local officials.

In light of what had happened, and considering what the girl had been through as well as her age, everyone had agreed that the adoption would be in her best interest.

Early on, Zoe realized that making Sarah believe that she was really wanted and loved, would take time. After all, she had lived through some very traumatic events. Asking for art classes was definitely a big step in the right direction.

A shy grin lit Sarah's typically solemn face. "Mr. Murray from school is teaching the classes. So, I already know him and," she looked uncharacteristically pleased with herself, "he says that I have real talent and just need a chance to immerse myself more in the type of art that I enjoy."

It was true—Sarah did have a talent for drawing and, more recently, for water-color painting.

Zoe was thrilled that her daughter's talent was being noticed and encouraged by her art teacher. She knew how much this meant to Sarah.

Kate, who already knew all about it, grinned. "See, Sarah, I knew she'd be all for it! Isn't it great, Mom?" she gushed as she patted Sarah on the back.

"Hey, I also heard that he's having a one-day art show and sale at the Currituck Lighthouse sometime in May. Tents and everything," she explained to her mother.

"You're going to have some things in that show too, aren't you, Sarah?"

Zoe smiled at them both. "This is all so exciting! I'll get you anything you need, Honey. Just let me know all the details when you find out."

Chapter 6

Hugh was gone and the girls were in bed when Zoe's cell phone rang and Rose's troubled voice asked, "Is Hugh over there, by chance? I need help."

"What's the matter, Rose?" Zoe sank into the closest chair. "Hugh just left, but he should be home in a minute and he has his cell phone with him. Do you need me to call an ambulance?"

"No, it's not like that." Rose hesitated and took a deep breath. "It's Susan, actually. She told me that she was going to her mother's house to sort through some things this evening, and well, she should have been home by now. But she's not.

"I mean she's not answering her cell phone and something must be wrong. You know," she continued, "that old house is just plain creepy on a good day."

"But, it also isn't like her to be this hard to get ahold of."

"Do you think Hugh would check on her for me? I'm afraid to go there by myself in case something has happened."

"I'll let him know right away, Rose, and I'm sure he'll head over there as fast as he can. Or would you rather call him, instead?

"You do it, Honey," she sounded relieved. "John and I are going to get in the car and head for the house right now."

"But I want Hugh to be there too, just in case something is...in case something has happened...well, you know," she lamely finished."

"Yes, I do know. Hey, Rose, let your husband do the driving, okay? Hopefully everything is alright, and maybe the cell-phone reception in that place is just bad. Do you want me to let you know when Hugh leaves?"

"No, we'll just meet him there." She hung up.

Zoe's hand shook slightly as she called Hugh. Fortunately, he answered on the first ring. "Hey, what's up, pretty lady? Do you miss me, already?"

The teasing note in his voice immediately evaporated when Zoe explained Rose's request for his help.

"Yeah, I'm heading out right now," he said, and turned back to his car.

Something between light rain and mist had begun to fall and the temperature was dropping. He shivered and propped the phone against his neck, and zipped up his jacket.

"I'll let you know what's happening as soon as I can." He turned on the squad car's flashing lights and carefully made his way back up the beach.

Even in an emergency, he would not let himself be a threat to the wild horses, nor to anyone else who might be out walking or driving in the dark, for that matter.

Once he reached the paved road, Hugh pushed the accelerator down. His gut-feeling was that something *was* wrong. It wasn't like Susan, who loved to talk, not to answer her calls. According to Zoe, she had been under some stress, too. Maybe she'd had a heart attack.

He managed to arrive at the house before Rose and her husband did. Susan's car sat close to the front door, and was illuminated by the interior lights that shone from the windows onto the wet ground.

He bounded up the steps and pounded on the door, but no one answered. He had called for police-backup on his way, and had also called for an ambulance, just in case.

42

Perhaps foolishly, without waiting for his backup to arrive, he decided to force the door, and drew his gun as he did so.

The bright chandelier revealed an empty hallway and he stood still for a moment, listening and looking around. But, all was quiet.

The living and dining room lights were on. He edged into the dining room first, where dust lay thickly on the furniture and where obviously, nothing had been disturbed. He lowered his gun for a moment, then raised it again as he carefully reentered the hall.

He figured that if anyone was hiding, they would either be in the back rooms or upstairs. But he needed to check the living room, first.

Hugh could see that Susan had been working in this room. Then he noticed an overturned chair and cautiously approached it, looking back over his shoulder as he did so, and that's when he saw her lying on the floor.

He wondered if she had lost her balance and fallen. He knelt next to her, but cautiously positioned himself to face the doorway so he wouldn't be vulnerable to anyone who might still be in the house.

He could see that she had struck her head against the edge of a small table when she'd fallen. Blood stained the corner of it, and was also trickling down the side of her head.

He stood up and grabbed a crocheted throw from the back of a nearby chair and covered her with it. Then he knelt again and checked her pulse. It was weak, but at least she was alive.

He pulled out his cell phone, hoping to intercept Rose and her husband because he didn't want them in the house in case it was a crime scene. But, he was too late.

Through the opened curtains, he saw the headlights of John's car pull up close to his own. Almost immediately behind them came an ambulance and two more police cars.

Hugh hurried to the door and directed the emergency staff into the living room, but he stepped in front of Rose as she hurried up the front steps right behind them. Her husband was close on her heels.

"Don't go in," he ordered. Rose sternly stared at him.

"She is my oldest friend, Hugh. Do you really think I'm not going into this house? And do you intend to stop me?" she fiercely asked.

Hugh gently but firmly took hold of her arm and turned her around. "Susan is unconscious, Rose, but I think she's going to be okay."

"I don't want you in the house just now because it may, or may not, be a crime scene. I haven't had a chance to look around, yet."

"There is a good possibility that she just fell off of a chair she was standing on. But there is also the possibility that someone else was here who pushed her."

"For all I know, they might still be in the house," he added. "I'm sure there are plenty of people who know that this house is empty. You know how news travels around here."

He forbore to mention that Rose and Susan were two of the reasons that news *did* travel so quickly around Corolla.

Rose pursed her lips and looked at her husband. Their eyes met and he nodded, and she relented with a sigh. "Okay, Hugh, have it your own way. But, I want you to call me the minute you know anything. Will you promise me that?"

"Absolutely," he agreed, and released her arm. "You do understand, don't you?"

"Reluctantly," she nodded, "but yes I do. We'll head back home. And," she looked him sternly in the eye, "I expect to hear from you within the hour."

"Yes, Ma'am," he touched the brim of his hat in a mocking salute. He watched them get into their car and drive away. Once the car's tail-lights were out of sight, he went back into the house.

The first thing he heard was Susan moaning and a man's voice reassuring her that she was going to be alright. That was surely a good sign, he thought. At least she was regaining consciousness.

He watched the EMTs carefully move her onto a gurney and went to hold the door for them.

"I know she fell," he said to a woman who was leaning over Susan, "but can you tell if she'd had a heart attack or any other medical problem that might have caused her to fall?"

Without looking up, the woman answered, "As near as we can tell, no. There is no evidence of anything else, but we'll have to see what the doctors say. They'll want to run a lot of tests."

As the ambulance pulled away, Hugh motioned to the officers who were waiting in the hall.

"Now that they've gone, let's take a look around. Someone else might still be in the house, so draw your guns and be careful."

However, a thorough search revealed only empty rooms. Hugh wanted to check for more evidence of an intruder, but decided to wait until morning to bring in the people to do that.

One of the young officers cleared his throat. "You know, Hugh, I grew up around here. When I was a kid, it was a big deal to ride our bikes over to the old Wellford place, and look for ghosts. It's not like we ever actually got to come inside though," he explained.

"Instead, we'd look through the windows and hide among the trees and bushes just in a case a ghost happened to leave the house." He grinned. "You know what kids are like."

"My point is that we grew up being told this place was haunted because at least one murder had happened here, long ago."

"At least that's what folks in this area always said. I always thought there was some truth to it because otherwise, why would people keep saying it?"

"Because they wanted to scare you into behaving yourselves?" Hugh snorted. "Like the boogey-man?"

He had gone back into the living room and looked up from where he was kneeling, near the over-turned chair.

"Just who was supposed to have been murdered here, Jimmy?" he asked.

"And when did it happen? I've lived here for ten years now, and I thought I'd heard all the local legends. But somehow, I missed this one."

The other officer spoke up. "Jimmy's right, sir. I grew up around here too, you see. My folks told my brothers and me to stay away from this place because there was a curse on it."

He chuckled. "Of course, being told that just made us want to come and explore, even more."

"We figured that if there were ghosts in the house, they might be worth seeing. Not that we ever made it into the house either," he quickly added.

"It's okay, Harper," Hugh grinned. "I'm not interested in arresting either you or Jimmy for breaking and entering here when you were kids."

Jimmy chuckled. "That's a relief! But as much as I'd like to brag that we broke in, we actually never did."

"Harper and I played together as kids and none of us ever had the nerve to even try it, though we dared each other to, from time to time."

"My folks also said there'd once been a murder here, and you didn't know who might still be hanging around the place, alive or dead."

Hugh stood up and folded his arms.

"That's interesting. It makes you wonder what's really up with this place."

"Before we leave, why don't you two look around outside and see if there are any prints or evidence of a ladder."

"I know you won't see much, even with flashlights, but it's still worth a quick look. By morning, any prints might disappear—on purpose or otherwise."

He held up a hand. "Before you do that though, can you tell me who was supposed to have been murdered here? And who supposedly put a curse on the family?"

"Honestly," Harper said, "nobody ever got around to telling us those details. I do know though, that my parents always kept a distance from the family, including Susan. They're a little younger than she is, but they all knew each other from school."

"Do you want me to ask them?" he added. "Maybe now that I'm grown-up, they'd be more willing to talk about it."

"Yeah," Hugh said. "I'd be interested in anything they have to say about it."

He shrugged. "Even the smallest details might help."

"I'll do the same," Jimmy said. "The truth is, I like Ms. Susan and I've got nothing against her."

"Besides, you can't be responsible for whatever your crazy family does, can you? So, as far as I'm concerned, whatever they did has nothing to do with her."

"I agree," Harper nodded. "But there will always be people who don't see it that way. It makes you wonder why she moved back here, and why she bothers to stay."

"Yes," Hugh agreed. "Then again, we don't really know her situation. She was married at one time, but her husband died and she came back. We'll need to find out where all she has lived, though."

"You never know," he explained, "she and her husband might have made at least one enemy, between them. Maybe somebody who has followed her here to do some damage." He cupped his chin thoughtfully.

Hugh felt that he had to check out every possibility. And anything that they were able to dig up might also explain why Susan needed Zoe's help.

Above all, he didn't want Zoe mixed up in anything dangerous.

Chapter 7

Susan awoke to find herself in a hospital room, in semi-darkness. The antiseptic smell was her first clue as to her location. For what seemed like a long time, she drifted in and out of consciousness, though in reality, it was only a few hours.

Her head hurt and she felt too heavy to move. In those moments when she was half-awake, she found that moving her eyes was painful and she would close them again.

Sometime in the night, she found it easier to keep her eyes open, and she also tried, somewhat successfully, to move.

She couldn't quite remember what had happened. It had something to do with a chair, but she found that trying to think made her head hurt worse, so she gave it up.

Instead, she fought the haziness and tried to focus. When she was finally able to look around without experiencing severe pain, she was more than a little surprised to see Hugh sitting in a chair that was pulled up close beside her bed.

He was reading a magazine, but looked up when she stirred and waited to see if she would drift off again. She worked hard not to, because she wanted to know what was going on.

"What happened, Hugh?" she croaked. Her hand lay on top of the blanket and he gently held it in both of his.

"As near as we can figure," he said, "you fell off a chair in your mother's house and hit your head on a table that was sitting nearby."

Susan closed her eyes and opened them again. She was suddenly dizzy, in spite of lying down. "What are the doctors saying about me?"

Hugh's hands tightened over hers as he leaned closer. "It's not too bad. In fact, they said it could have been a whole lot worse."

"You have a concussion and you've lost a little blood, but overall, you're not in bad shape and they expect you to fully recover."

"But," he added, "You'll be staying here overnight and maybe tomorrow, so they can keep an eye on you."

"You've been drifting in and out of consciousness, and the nurses are regularly checking on you. They're taking good care of you here, Susan."

She frowned. "I vaguely recall people talking to me and wanting me to answer them, but I thought I was dreaming."

An uneasy look crossed her face and she suddenly gripped his hands tightly.

"Did I talk in my sleep?" she asked. "What did I say?"

"Nothing too exciting, as far as I know," he reassured her. "But you have been muttering off and on since I've been sitting here with you, too. And, that's what concerns me."

"You are clearly afraid of something or someone. Will you tell me what, so that I can help you?"

She pursed her lips. Her face was as white as her sheets except for the large, purplish bruise on the left side of her head.

She'd gone quiet and Hugh didn't want to upset her, so he changed the subject.

"Zoe wanted to come and stay with you, but since it's so late, I told her that I'd stay myself, just to make sure that you were doing okay."

"And, I sent Rose and John home, too. None of us wanted you to wake up alone."

"You're all so good to me." Tears flooded Susan's cheeks. "Believe me, I don't deserve to have such good friends."

Hugh grabbed a box of tissues from the nightstand and sat it on the bed next to her.

"I feel like such a fool for crying," she sobbed.

"It's okay," his voice was soothing. "You've been through a lot and you're very weak right now. But everything is going to be just fine."

He added, "We're your friends. We think the world of you, Susan. Zoe and Rose will tell you so themselves when they get here in the morning. Meanwhile, I'm not going anywhere."

Susan took a couple of deep breaths and painfully blew her nose. The result was that her head felt as though it might explode.

"That means more to me than you can possibly know, Hugh," she finally said. "Please tell me exactly what I did say when I was unconscious. I need to know."

"Well," he thought for a moment, "like I said, nothing too spectacular."

"You said that someone was after you and you didn't know who it was. It's possible that you were just been dreaming. I wanted to check with you, just in case."

She gently pulled her hand away from his and closed her eyes.

"I don't honestly believe that anyone is out to get me. So, maybe you're right and I was just dreaming about something."

She lay quietly for a little while then confessed, "Even as a little girl, I always had the feeling that someone was watching me in that house, so maybe my childhood fears came back while I was unconscious."

51

"I need to rest now, Hugh." You don't have to stay here; go on home and get to bed. I'll be fine and I'll see you all tomorrow."

"You go to sleep, Susan. I'm going to stay a while yet," he reassured her.

Chapter 8

A vivid sunrise colored a swath of the ocean in shades of deep rose and gold the next morning.

But that was nature, wasn't it, Zoe reflected. Life goes on as usual, no matter what happens. It seemed to her that when circumstances shattered one's world, time should stand still.

"At such times, thunder and lightning should split the sky," she said to herself.

She pushed open her bedroom window to let in the cold, salty wind, and took a deep breath. Her house sat near the ocean in one of the most beautiful places imaginable.

Some people would find the location too remote. But she and Kate, and Sarah, loved it.

Reluctantly, she turned away and picked up her cell-phone. First, she needed an update on Susan's condition, and then she had to fix breakfast and drop the girls off at school.

She wondered how much sleep Hugh had managed to get.

Before she could ring him up though, he called to fill her in on Susan's progress. He said that he'd left the hospital a couple of hours earlier to go home and shower and change his clothes.

"I need to leave here again in about 15 minutes," he said. "Do you want me to drop the girls off, on my way?"

"No," she answered, "but, thanks anyway. I'm going to stop in to see Susan, and then I have an appointment with the director of that new museum in Duck."

"I might stop by the local historical society, too, if there's time."

They were both in a hurry, but Hugh seemed reluctant to hang up, so Zoe waited. But when he didn't say anything more, she asked, "Is everything okay?"

"I'm concerned about you having to go to work when you've already been awake most of the night."

"No, I'm fine," he reassured her. "I actually slept sitting in the chair in Susan's room. He added, "It wouldn't be the first time that I've had to get by on very little sleep. That seems to be part of my job description, at least from time to time."

"But hopefully not too often," she sympathized.

"Hey, Zoe, when you see Susan today, don't push her to tell you anything about her house, or her family, or whatever happened to her last night."

"The truth is she's pretty fragile right now. And there may be nothing more to the story than the fact that she doesn't know what to do with the house, and she fell off that chair. So just go easy on her, okay?"

Zoe sighed. "I will admit that I have a tendency to be impatient, but that's because I *do* want to help her."

"However, I solemnly swear that I will not push her for information. At least not for the time being."

Hugh laughed. "You're a good woman, Zoe, and one of the best-hearted people I know. But you're not always patient. And I'm pretty sure that this situation is going to require patience from all of us."

A little later, at the hospital, Zoe tactfully limited her conversation to the weather and the local gossip as chiefly related to her by Rose, from whose personal radar, not much news escaped.

Then again, the people who typically shopped in her store were not opposed to lingering over a cup of coffee and a chat whenever they stopped by, either. So, it was only natural that she would stay informed.

By the time Zoe was standing up to leave, Rose breezed in carrying flowers and a paper bag in one hand, and her large, shell-print handbag in the other.

"John is minding the store today," she explained. "Heaven knows he has no clue where anything is located should anyone ask, but he'll just have to get by."

"It's more important for me to be here." She leaned over and patted Susan's shoulder.

"How are you feeling this morning, Honey? Are they taking good care of you?"

Susan affirmed that they were, and Rose turned to Zoe. "Thanks for getting Hugh onto it right away last night."

"You let me know how your interview goes, okay?" She settled herself in the chair that Zoe had just vacated.

Outside, the spring sunshine and fresh air felt especially good after the semi-darkness and antiseptic smells of the hospital.

Zoe cautiously pulled out onto Route 12 and headed west for her interview with Stephen Barnum, the director of The Outer Banks Cultural Museum.

If all went well, she would work as a consultant for the organization, helping with research and design.

Based on her telephone conversation with him, Stephen wanted to take the scope of the Outer Banks history back to the year dot, which was very likely impossible, at least with any amount of accuracy.

Nevertheless, she was looking forward to getting back to work, again. And being in on the creation of a new museum was an exciting prospect.

The minute she climbed out of her Jeep, a tall, middle-aged man with dark, curly hair and a broad smile opened the front door of the elegant-looking building she'd parked in front of.

He gestured broadly to her to come inside, and then waved his arm around the foyer in a theatrical, sweeping gesture.

"Well, what do you think, so far?" He eagerly asked.

Without waiting for an answer, he led her through a series of clean, brightly-lit rooms whose walls varied from highly polished wood to sea-worn siding.

Empty cases were randomly shoved against walls, waiting to be moved into their final positions and filled with artifacts.

Finally, they reached Stephen Barnham's office and he ushered her in with another dramatic flourish.

"Would you like tea or coffee?" he paused with one hand on the door and shouted to someone named Jesse to bring coffee for two.

Then he sank down in a leather chair behind his desk and waved her into a plush one, opposite.

A few moments later, a tall, elegant woman entered with a tray of cups and saucers as well as a coffee pot, which she carefully placed on the desk. She poured out a cup for each of them.

"Thank you, Jesse," Stephen smiled. "I'd like you to meet Zoe Hamilton, who is hopefully coming to help us out as a consultant. She was a curator in Virginia and she knows her stuff."

The woman smiled and extended her hand. "I'm glad to meet you, Zoe. I'm Jesse Longstreet and I'm actually the staff archeologist.

But at the moment, as you can see, I am serving as Stephen's general dogs-body." Her smile broadened as his face went bright-red and he rose to the bait.

"That's not true!" he shouted. "You just happen to make better coffee than anyone else here, including me."

She grimaced. "We'll talk about that later, Stephen. Meanwhile, I'll leave you to it. See you around, Zoe," she grinned.

He carefully sipped his coffee and sat the cup back down while Zoe wondered if the staff regularly enjoyed winding him up. Jesse clearly did, and he seemed to be an easy enough target.

"We are so excited about your coming to help us," Stephen gushed, which made Zoe inadvertently squirm.

The more he talked though, the more she realized that he was no fool. Instead, he was a very shrewd man who seemed to know exactly how to get what he wanted.

Among other accomplishments, he had somehow managed to secure all of the museum's required funding for the next five years. She had never known anyone before who could pull that off.

In the end, she agreed to sign on as a consultant. Even more important, at least to her, was the fact that she successfully negotiated for the salary and terms that she wanted.

"I'll have your contract drawn up right away," Stephen promised. "We should have it by next week at the latest and hopefully, even sooner. Our attorneys know that we're in a hurry. I want this done quickly."

He slapped a large hand down on top of his desk and made her jump.

"Now!" he shouted with an expansive grin, "Do you have any other questions for me?"

"Only one," her voice seemed unusually quiet compared to his, "and it's completely irrelevant to the work, here." Stephen frowned.

"Do you know a local woman named Susan Hall? Or more to the point, do you happen to know anything about her family, the Wellfords?

She owns a rather grand, old family home in Corolla that backs up to the Sound."

"Wellford," he mused as he carefully put the tips of his fingers together. "The name doesn't ring a bell, for some reason. But you know, I grew up in Duck and it's not that far away, so I must have been aware of the family.

Then again, I was gone from here for about 25 years, so it may be that I simply don't remember."

His frown deepened. "I'm going to have to think about it further, because nothing is coming to me." She rose to leave, and he slowly rose to his feet, as well.

"If I remember anything, I'll let you know, "he promised. Is it urgent?"

"Not really," she answered.

Chapter 9

There were several historical societies in the area, but Zoe wanted one that specifically focused on Corolla.

That one sat on a quiet, side-street surrounded by tall pines and numerous rose bushes, the latter of which leaned in abundance against the building.

As Zoe pulled open a Victorian-type screen door, she nearly collided with a petite, dark-haired young woman who was gripping the handle from the other side.

"I am *so* sorry! I was just going out to water the ferns," she said. We don't usually make a habit of knocking our visitors down, you know."

"No problem," Zoe smiled and extended her hand. "I should have looked more closely before I pulled on the door."

"I'm Zoe Hamilton. I'll be working as a consultant for the museum in Duck, so I wanted to come by and introduce myself to you. We will probably be exchanging information from time to time."

The dark-haired woman beamed as she took Zoe's outstretched hand. "In that case, I really am glad to meet you and even more sorry about the door."

She motioned at Zoe to follow her inside. "Has Mr. Barnum decided on an opening date, yet?"

"Not as far as I know," Zoe said. A date had been mentioned, but nothing had been made public, yet.

"I'll let you know as soon as I find out," she promised.

The woman nodded. "Great! I'm Renee Lloyd, by the way. Do you have time to sit down for a few minutes so we can get acquainted?"

She pointed at two blue-and-white easy chairs that sat side-by-side. "I'm sure we'll be seeing a lot of each other in the not-too-distant future."

Two end tables sat near the chairs, and there was also a dark-blue couch and a coffee table that faced a large, stone fireplace. Blooming African violets sat on the fireplace mantle.

"What a beautiful room," Zoe told her, and meant it. It was inviting and comfortable, and somehow, also soothing.

Renee looked pleased. "Thank you!"

"Some people think that I'm overly-fussy, but if you can make a room both inviting and functional, why wouldn't you do that?"

Zoe agreed and silently wondered if it would be appropriate to ask Renee for some personal decorating advice, then decided she shouldn't—at least not until they knew each other better.

And instant later, Renee pulled her attention back to the moment. "Zoe, if you have any extra time, would you consider helping us here, too?"

"We're always looking for good volunteers, but I think we might be able to offer you a paid position. And your experience would be valuable to us."

Zoe was surprised, but pleased. "We might be able to work something out," she said.

"My schedule with Stephen Barnham will vary, so if you can work with that, then I see no reason why I can't help out here, too."

"Excellent!" Renee clapped her hands. "I'm meeting with our Board of Directors today and will need their approval, but I'm sure there will be no problem."

"If you don't mind giving me your phone number, I'll get back to you later this afternoon."

"By the way," she added, "since I'm sure that we will be working together, I'll tell you up-front that we need some good ideas for a fund-raiser, as soon as possible.

"I want it to be a major, community event. Would you be willing to help with that?"

"Absolutely," Zoe said. "I've worked on quite a few events in the past, including fund-raisers. I'll help you as much as I can."

"I also have a confession to make," she added. "The other reason I came by, is to ask if you, or anyone here, knows Susan Hall. Her family name was Wellford and the family lived in this area for ages. Susan moved away, but came back a few years ago."

"I know who she is, but I've never actually spoken with her," Renee said.

"The good news, she added, "is that the Historical Society does have some information about the Wellford family."

"Would you like to look while you're here? Oddly enough, I was just reading up on that house," she said thoughtfully. "The family was definitely wealthy and prominent, at one time."

Zoe followed Renee to her office.
"I can take a look at what's on file for you. We usually take requests for information and do the research ourselves because, as you know, a lot can be damaged or go missing."

"But since you'll be working with us, you're welcome to peruse whatever we have."

"Besides which," she added, "you'll want to take a look at our archival-room, anyway."

Zoe followed her further up the hall and they stopped in front of a door with a keypad. Renee pushed in the correct numbers and opened the door.

The room was entirely filled with boxes, some of which were organized on shelves while others sat in groups on the floor, waiting to be organized.

Fortunately, most of them were numbered and dated, and Renee pointed at a stack that sat against the opposite wall.

"That group is where you'll want to begin," she said. "You're welcome to either look at them now, or come back whenever you want."

Zoe glanced at her watch. "I can stay a little while." She had a couple of hours before she needed to pick up the girls from school.

"I'd be interested to know what you find out about the family and their house," she added.

Renee's dark eyes focused momentarily on the far wall. "There are old, local stories about the Wellfords, as well as their house, to tell you the truth," she said.

"But of course, you only want the facts, don't you? As I'm sure you know, stories are so easily embroidered over time, and personally, I don't put much faith in them."

"Yes, of course," Zoe agreed, hoping that Renee would share some of those stores with her. However far-fetched they might be, they might also contain some truth that would help round out the facts she was seeking.

"I'll take a quick look here and see what I can turn up. You know, Susan is thinking of either renting or selling the old family home."

"Really? I hadn't heard that." She flashed a brilliant smile. "That place would be a treasure for someone to live in. Meanwhile, I'll be in my office, if you need me."

With a sigh, Zoe folded her jacket and laid it on top of one of the cleaner-looking boxes, nearby. 'Treasure' wasn't exactly the word she would have used to describe that cold house.

She opened a box marked "Wellford" and was surprised to see a stack of papers on top, covered with faded, spidery writing.

Surely these should be in an acid-free folder, she thought. But at least the box, itself, was acid free. Maybe the staff hadn't completed their sorting, yet.

And, at least for the present, storage issues at the historical society were not her problem.

Unfortunately, her search failed to uncover any dark, family mysteries and Zoe resigned herself to copying dates and names from the family tree. If only she had come across something significant to tell Hugh.

At least she was learning something about the Wellfords and their impact on the community, though. Maybe at some point it would all fit together and solve the puzzle.

They had owned a general store in Corolla that later included a post office, and were a prosperous family, but that much was obvious anyway.

One interesting point that Zoe discovered was that Susan had an older brother named Simon. Where was he, she wondered.

Meanwhile, having done all that she could for the present, Zoe buttoned her jacket, picked up her notebook, and asked herself if

Susan had really fallen off that chair. Beautiful as it was, the Wellford house was creepy.

As far as she knew, there was no actual proof that anyone else had been in the house, at the time. Hugh thought it was a possibility, but he hadn't said anything more, so presumably no evidence had been found.

Renee might know more than she was saying, but then again, maybe not.

Meanwhile, Rose would undoubtedly have an opinion, and would be more than happy to share her thoughts.

Zoe pulled the door closed and waved at Renee as she passed her office.

"Did you find anything?" Renee called and then stood up.

"Hey, before you go, I want you to meet Ella Radcliffe. She's an old-timer here in Corolla, and I was just telling her about your coming to help us out."

Ella stood just inside the door of Renee's office. She was a thin, wiry-looking woman with white, curly hair who was perhaps, in her 70s. It was hard to tell. She pushed her glasses farther up her nose.

"I'm glad to hear that you'll be working with us," she coolly said as her eyes held Zoe's.

"I also hear that you've been looking through some of the Wellford boxes."

A sudden, malicious glint lit her eyes and instantly disappeared. Had Zoe imagined it?

She looked sharply at the older woman, whose expression was now carefully bland.

"As it happens," Ella said, "I know Susan quite well." She brushed an invisible speck of dust from the sleeve of her yellow sweater.

"I went all the way through school with her, you know. I also know something about that house, or at least what people were saying about that house back when we were young."

The malicious glint returned and was gone in an instant. This time, Zoe was sure of it. She glanced at her watch, and sat down.

Chapter 10

On her way home, Zoe stopped by the hospital to see Susan again, and learned that she was scheduled to be released the following morning.

Rose was going to pick her up and spend the day with her while her husband, John, took care of the store again.

Susan was obviously pleased to know she was going home, but participating in conversation still seemed to be a great effort for her.

"I'm fine," she kept repeating, "but I'm just so tired." Rose had spent the day at the hospital with her, and Zoe wondered if Susan hadn't rested enough. Then again, maybe having Rose with her made up for not getting enough rest.

Later, at home, Zoe told Kate, "I telephoned the Wild Horse Fund this morning and asked if they would consider bringing you on as a volunteer."

Kate's eyes widened and she abruptly sat her drink on the counter.

"And, they agreed," Zoe finished. "So, if you really want to do this, I'll make sure that you can get back and forth, as needed."

Kate threw her arms around her mother's neck, and nearly toppled them both over in the process. She had grown almost as tall as Zoe, and was certainly as strong.

Kate dearly loved the wild horses and had, early-on, wanted to be involved with the organization that protected them. When she was older, she hoped to actually work with the herd, too. But meanwhile, this was a step in the right direction.

She grabbed two protein bars from the cupboard for herself and Sarah, and they both headed upstairs to change their clothes just as Hugh pushed open the front door.

The wind had picked up, and sand and the evening mist obscured the darkening sky outside.

"That's quite a wind," he observed. "From the look of it, I think we're in for a storm later on. Hopefully no tornadoes, though."

He headed for the kitchen, but Zoe managed to waylay him in the living room, and gripped his arm.

"I need to talk to you without the girls around." She looked unusually serious, and the smile slowly drained from his face as he reached for her hand and led her to the couch.

"What is it?" He sounded more like a law-enforcement officer than a lover.

"Are you and the girls alright?"

"We're fine," she waved away his inquiries. "It's nothing to do with us."

"I've been talking to a woman named Ella Radcliffe who works with the local historical society. She knows Susan. She claims they went to school together."

"Is that a problem?" He looked puzzled. "I'm sure there are still quite a few people around here who either went to school with Susan or at least know her, and you did want to find out more, right?"

Zoe tapped her foot impatiently. "Would you like to hear what she had to say, or shall I not bother to tell you?"

"Wait just a minute," he stopped her. "Before you repeat anything this woman said, keep in mind that it may not be the gospel-truth. You do know that, don't you?"

Zoe's head reared back and her green eyes narrowed. "Do I look like an idiot, Hugh? Of course I don't believe everything I hear," she snorted.

She jumped to her feet, but he still held her hand and pulled her back down.

"I know that, Sweetheart, "he said soothingly. "But, I can't help thinking that you've heard the worst, and the worst may not even be true. And worst of all," he played with the word, "is the possibility that whatever you've heard will make you doubt Susan."

"She really is a good person, Zoe. I don't want to have to convince you of that a second time."

"Actually," she leaned away from him and coolly replied, "It's not Susan that I doubt. It's her family, which isn't quite the same thing, is it. What do you know about them?"

"Not much, so far," he admitted. "I've lived here a while, but I'm not an old-timer. And people tend to not confess much of anything to police officers anyway, unless they're either under stress or oath. It's just one of the many perks of doing this kind of work," he joked.

Zoe, who was not in the mood to be amused, ignored this remark.

"I was going to tell you what Ella said, but if you're not interested, that's fine. I need to finish dinner, anyway."

Once again, she made a move to get up and Hugh tightened his grip on her hand. He slid to the edge of the couch and gripped her shoulders, and looked directly into her eyes.

"Listen, my love, I want to hear anything that you have to say to me. But, you're so quick to be angry sometimes, and I have to wonder if you do it deliberately just to push me away."

"Zoe, you know that I love you and I'll marry you the moment that you agree to it, no matter what. But I can't always read you and I don't always understand what's going on in your head."

"I just wish that you could trust me instead of jumping on me over nothing much, sometimes."

Zoe sighed. "I don't know why I do it, Hugh. But," she drew in a deep breath and released it, "I have no doubt that you're right and I really am sorry. I need to think about this, and we need to talk about it some more."

"Right now, before the girls come back downstairs, I need to tell you what I learned about Susan's family."

She looked away for a moment, then met his eyes. "As far as you and I are concerned, I do love you. I don't know why I'm impatient sometimes, but I do know the problem is not you. It's me."

Hugh sighed and leaned back against the cushions. "Okay, Zoe," he said.

"The sad thing is that whenever you're ready and will have me, I'll still be right here. I'm not much of a tough guy after all, am I?" He shook his head.

She covered his hand with hers and said, "Believe me, you're really not the problem, Hugh. You're one of the best people I've ever known, and maybe that's what frightens me."

"I've never known anyone quite like you. I guess I'm just scared that you're too good to be true."

"I am," he solemnly said. "I am too good to be true." She playfully slapped his arm.

"Be serious! I want to know if what I heard today is true. Because whether it is or not, we need to figure out how best to help her, and this might shine some light on the situation."

They were interrupted at that moment by the girls who had come back downstairs for dinner.

Chapter 11

They ate chili with corn bread and afterward, gathered in front of the television with large mugs of hot chocolate topped with whipped cream.

They looked like an advertisement for happy family spending an evening together, and Zoe wondered if she could ever allow herself to make that a reality.

Later, once the girls were upstairs finishing their homework and catching up on each other's news, Hugh turned on the gas fireplace and patted the cushion beside him on the couch.

This time, Zoe sat close to him and rested her head on his shoulder while his arm tightened around her. "Are you ready?" she asked. He nodded.

"Okay," she sighed. "In a way, it's not much, but in a way, it is. And, it does explain some things."

"By the way, Ella says the house has had a reputation for being haunted, for many years now."

"That much, I did know," Hugh murmured against her hair. She sat up.

"What else do you know? I thought you said you didn't know anything."

"I don't, really," he answered as he reached out and gently stroked her hair. "And what I do know, I only found out by accident."

"A couple of the guys said that, as kids, they'd been forbidden to go near the place because it was haunted, and I don't know what else."

"Of course, you know how that worked out—it ensured that they hung around there anyway," he chuckled.

Zoe looked thoughtful. "Well, according to some of the locals, there are several ghosts residing in that house. Some, or maybe all of them, were victims of one of Susan's great grandfathers—I'm not sure how many 'greats' back that is," she added.

"But, the family has evidently lived in the Outer Banks since close to the beginning of time, according to Ella."

"I'm sure you also know there have been a lot of ship-wrecks along this shore. Most of them, and maybe all of them, were legitimate wrecks. When they happened, it seems that pretty much everyone tried to help rescue the crew, the passengers, and whatever cargo there was."

"But now and then, someone would help themselves to some of the cargo," she explained, "especially if it was lumber or something useful like that."

"Apparently," she continued, "there was a time when one of Susan's great-grandfathers collaborated with three other men to grab whatever they could from the wrecks, while the others were busy rescuing people, and livestock, and cargo."

"Ella said they managed to keep a horse and wagon handy, and a couple of the men would carry off what they could while the other two pitched in and helped with the rescue, to help keep everyone else distracted."

"Most of this was done when the ships wrecked at night. I mean," she added, "it would be a lot harder to pull off something like that in broad daylight, wouldn't it?"

"Anyway, the story goes that Susan's great-grandfather, Cyrus Wellford, decided, at some point, to double-cross his partners by not sharing all of the money that he made from selling the stolen goods."

"Eventually, the men grew suspicious and one fateful night, they decided to confront him at his home, which at that time, was around Hatteras. He supposedly had a good-sized barn on his property where everything they stole, was stored."

"Oh, well, that was convenient," Hugh interjected. "I see where this is going."

"Based on my observations, you don't double-cross your partners-in-crime and then think that everything is going to work out okay for you."

"Yes," she nodded in agreement. "Well, it didn't. Old Cyrus figured out that it was only a matter of time until they would suspect him, so he started carrying a gun."

"On that dark, moonless night, following the latest wreck, the men demanded to see just how much of their 'inventory' had been sold, so that they could calculate whether or not they had been cheated."

"As you can imagine, Cyrus refused. At first, he tried to bluff his way out of it, and then finally pulled out his gun and shot one of the men."

"The other two ran, but they couldn't get away fast enough in the dark and Cyrus caught up with them. He shot one and stabbed the other to death."

"That's a pretty story," Hugh snorted. "You know, like in any tight-knit community, people don't forget what other people do. Those memories tend to live on for a very long time."

"So, what happened to Cyrus, then? Did he hang for his crimes?"

"No, as a matter of fact, he didn't." Zoe sat up and ran a hand through her hair.

"There wasn't enough proof because there were no bodies. The dead men just happened to disappear, which means that he probably dragged them into a boat, took them out to the sea, and dumped them."

"Anyway, no one could prove anything, but the people were up-in-arms about it, anyway."

"Cyrus, who wasn't a stupid man, hastily moved farther north. But," she added, "I think it was actually his son who settled in Corolla."

"By that time, the family had quite a lot of money—possibly from the wrecks, but who knows? Maybe they came by some of it honestly."

"Ella told me that Cyrus's son was a prosperous storekeeper around here, but was reputed to be none-too-honest, either."

"He also ran small cargo ships along the coast, and I would imagine there was good money in that," she added.

"I would think so," Hugh agreed. "Always plenty of things to move. But, at least those businesses are legal and hopefully didn't include killing people."

"So, Susan's family goes back a few generations here, in this area," he said thoughtfully. "And no doubt the story followed them and has stuck like glue, ever since."

They were both quiet for a while, and then Hugh said, " 'Old sins cast long shadows.' I don't remember where I heard that, but it's certainly true in places like this where everyone pretty-much knows everyone else's history and business."

"That would also explain why Susan doesn't want to draw attention to her family's home," he added.

"Yes, but that's not all," Zoe said. "Ella couldn't recall the details, but there were some scandals involving both Susan's grandfather and her father, as well. So even if some of this is true, it explains a lot. But, we still don't know all of it."

Hugh stretched his arms and yawned. "They might also have been 'guilty by association' instead of in reality, you know."

"I'll see if I can confirm any of what Ella told you. It's a good starting point. Meanwhile," he added, "don't say anything to Susan about this. I don't think she's up to it."

"I won't," Zoe agreed. "But I wonder why she came back to this place after her husband died. It doesn't seem to make sense, does it?"

"No," he said. "But, we don't know all of it. There might have been a very good reason. I'll see what I can find out. Meanwhile, don't offer her any ideas about how to raise money, okay?"

"Why?" she asked "What difference can that possibly make?"

"I don't know," he said. "I'm just being cautious. I want to be sure that she really wants the money to do something about her house, and that there's not another reason."

"Such as what?" Zoe demanded.

"I honestly don't know," he admitted. "But until I know that, I'd rather you didn't get too personally involved. You're a new-comer here and you're trying..." he corrected himself, "...we're trying to make a home here, if you'll ever have me."

"I just don't want you taking any heat from the prejudice that other people might have toward her."

Zoe looked at him in surprise. Hugh was the last person who would advise her to abandon a good friend in need.

He seemed to assume that she agreed with him, because he abruptly changed the subject and talked about a benefit concert that he wanted to take her to, on Saturday night.

Privately, Zoe didn't see why she shouldn't help Susan, regardless of what anyone thought.

Chapter 12

The next morning, Zoe stopped by The Old Village Store to see Rose before she left to pick up Susan.

The Store opened at the early hour of 7 a.m. and surprisingly, did a decent amount of business.

As usual, the coffee was ready. Zoe was the first to arrive and Rose handed her a full cup without asking if she wanted one. She did.

They leisurely chatted as others came in, and Zoe lingered until they finally had the place to themselves, again.

"What are you up to, Honey?" Rose's eyes narrowed. "It's not like you to hang around here this early when you have to get the girls to school. What's on your mind?"

"The girls are riding in with Gwen Wilkens today, so I can take my time," Zoe informed her.

"In that case, let me refill your cup," Rose offered. "But that still doesn't answer my question, does it? Now what's going on?"

Zoe grinned. "Okay, I give up. I'm just not cut out to live a life of intrigue and deceit."

"That's not a bad thing, Honey," Rose remarked as she sank into her armchair near the counter.

"Come on, we're friends. Tell me what you're up to."

Zoe took a deep breath. "I want to ask you a couple of questions, but I'm not sure how to approach them."

"My advice is to just ask," Rose said. Fire away."

"What do you think happened to Susan the night she fell? I mean, do you think she might have been pushed?"

Rose stared down at her cup for a moment, then got up and refilled it.

Once she'd sat back down, she said, "I think Susan fell off her chair. I know Hugh has this whole theory about someone else being in the house, but I doubt it."

"Susan and I aren't getting any younger and she just lost her balance, that's all. And it wasn't any family spooks that did it, either," she half-joked.

"That house is spooky enough that I'm not saying there aren't any ghosts in there. In fact, if ghosts really exist, then that house is everything they could ever hope for, and then some." She shook her head. "But Susan just fell, that's all."

Zoe was deep in thought when Rose asked, "What else you want to know?"

"Do you know that Susan has a brother?"

Rose looked startled. "Well, of course I do. But how do you know about him? Did Susan say something?"

"No, Zoe admitted. "I saw his name somewhere. I just want to help her, Rose."

Rose pursed her lips and Zoe wondered if she'd intruded into something she shouldn't have.

"Simon Wellford ran away from home at the young age of 16 and no one heard anything about him after that, though his family did what they could to try and trace him," Rose finally said.

"He wanted to get away from them, you see. He was older than Susan."

She ran her hand across her eyes. "I am too sleepy this morning. I'll have to go pick up Susan soon, but I'll tell you the rest of it, first."

"About 15 years after Simon left, Susan got word that he'd died in a car crash. The good news was that he had hired an attorney who was instructed to contact his sister if he should die, and they eventually tracked her down. And that's all I know."

"Thanks, Rose," Zoe said. "Please give Susan my love and tell her I'll stop by later to see how she's doing."

Chapter 13

By the time Susan left the hospital, she was distinctly embarrassed about having fallen off a chair. She didn't want people to think that she was so feeble, she couldn't keep her balance.

What bothered her most though, was her belief that she had been pushed. And no ghost had done it, either. She was almost sure that she had felt someone's hands on her before she fell.

Hugh said that they didn't found any evidence of forced entry, and no one else had a key, as far as she knew. Then again, maybe people broke into houses without leaving clues, sometimes.

She moved her reading glasses farther up her nose and considered that the last thing she needed just now was another complication. And a potentially deadly one, at that.

Strangely, neither Rose nor Zoe had pressed her for details about her accident, and she had seen quite a lot of both of them over the past couple of days.

She wondered what her late husband would have made of all of this, and what he would have advised her to do. They had met forty years ago at a party and had lived happily ever after.

But everything, good and bad, eventually ends. When Frank Hall unexpectedly died, Susan sold their home in Raleigh and moved back to Corolla, to make a new start.

Most of all, she was homesick for the sea and the way of life on the Outer Banks. But maybe she had been too optimistic about coming home. Some old-timers still managed to avoid her like the plague.

Fortunately, other people didn't. Who could possibly hate her enough to want her dead, though? She couldn't think of any likely candidates, even among those who avoided her.

Susan's cell phone suddenly chimed. It was Zoe.

"Susan!" she all but shouted. "I have good news! But I want to tell you in person, so I'll be there in about five minutes if that's okay."

She managed to make it in three, and burst through the door bringing the cold, ocean wind with her.

Susan led the way to the kitchen and poured them each a cup of coffee while Zoe pulled out a chair. "Want some cream or sugar with that?" she asked.

Zoe impatiently gestured at the cream pitcher. "I had some earlier, so I can only drink one more cup."

"Have you, by chance, met Renee Lloyd who heads up the Corolla Historical Society?"

Susan shook her head, and Zoe continued. "As you know, I'm going to be a consultant there, too. But I heard from her early this morning, and she has come up with a wonderful plan for a fundraiser!"

Zoe grinned. "She's going to bring a Renaissance Faire here, to Corolla. Isn't that wonderful?"

Susan frowned. "I went to a Renaissance Faire many years ago," she said.

"It was over in Ashville and it was beautiful. All the costumes and the things people were selling, and the plays and other entertainment. There were even knights on horses, jousting. Great, powerful-looking horses, as I recall."

"Yes," Zoe said. "The food is usually pretty good too as I recall, though I haven't been to a Renaissance Faire since I was in college, years ago."

Susan's frown deepened. "How did Renee come up with something like that?"

"Well," Zoe explained, "One of her friends over in Raleigh suggested it. Apparently, he's done it before to raise money, and told her it was very successful. People came from all over and everyone made a lot of money," she said.

Susan waited, wondering why Zoe had come running so quickly to tell her about this.

"The point is," she continued, "Renee has already contacted a Renaissance group who is willing to come here in May."

"But here is the thing," she beamed, "We need a place to hold the Faire."

Susan still looked puzzled. "Well, where *are* you going to hold it? You'd need quite a lot of space, and also a road to make it accessible to the public."

"I shouldn't think there are too many places around here that would accommodate anything as large as a Renaissance Faire."

Zoe's impatience was bringing her close to a bursting point.

"Yes, Susan," she agreed. "That's just it, you see! We want to use your property. Your family home," she explained.

"You have five acres on Currituck Sound that would be perfect. And best of all," she added, "You would be paid a lot of money for the use of your land."

Susan sat with her mouth open for a moment, then finally said, "But, what about the money for the historical society? How can they afford to pay rent to me?"

"This is one of those situations when money has to be spent in order to make more money," Zoe explained.

"They have the money to pay you, and what they're paying you will go a long way toward getting the repairs made to your house."

Susan looked down at her tightly clenched hands. A surge of relief flowed over her like warm, salt-water.

"Yes," her voice quavered for a moment.

Zoe managed to find a couple of clean tissues in her handbag and pushed them across the table. She hadn't expected Susan to cry and went to put her arm around the older woman.

When Susan could finally speak again, she waved a tissue and said, "I really can't thank you enough, you know. You have just saved my life."

"The best part is that this will make everyone happy," Zoe told her. "I knew we would come up with something." She sat down again and took a sip of coffee.

"I don't mean to rush you, because you've been through a lot. But we need to discuss the business side of this, soon."

"You will need to sign a contract and there are insurance issues to sort out, but those are not your problem. The Historical Society will accept all responsibility."

She said excitedly, "There are also some legal issues to sort out with the county, but Renee will handle all of those."

"It shouldn't be a problem. A lot of people around here support the Historical Society and besides, the Renaissance Faire will bring in a lot of money to local hotels and shops."

"I was just wondering about that," Susan said. "Won't the local businesses be upset by people shopping and eating at the Faire instead of at their places?"

"We don't think it will be a problem," Zoe said. "In the first place, the Faire will only be here for a week, but their presence will attract even more people to the area."

"Also, most visitors will want to experience the local, Outer Banks shops and restaurants, as well as the Faire."

She swallowed the rest of her coffee and briskly said, "Now, if you have time and are feeling up to it, let's drive over and take a good look at your property so we can decide on the best site."

"It doesn't need to be on your door-step, and I want you to be comfortable with the set-up."

Susan pushed back her chair. "I am so excited that I could probably run all the way from here to there, to tell you the truth. As long as I get the money I need, they can set up that Faire anywhere they want."

Zoe laughed. "You might think differently about that after a day or so of having them right on your doorstep."

Chapter 14

"The Renaissance Faire will begin on the second weekend in May," Zoe informed Hugh later that afternoon. She couldn't wait to tell him, but he was obviously not pleased, as indicated by his deep groan and raised eyebrows.

"Why aren't you happy about this?" she asked, as she got up to refill his water glass.

"Here, try one of these brownies. They turned out really well, if I do say so myself." She frowned and sat the entire pan down in front of him.

"I thought that, at the least, you would be pleased for Susan," she said. "It's not like there are a lot of money-raising options, you know. Not on that scale, anyway." She snatched up a brownie and bit into it.

Hugh met her eyes. "I *am* happy for Susan, but not quite so happy for the rest of us, Zoe."

"I know about these Faires and, believe me they can create a lot of problems."

Zoe looked past him and out of the window where the evening clouds darkened over the silver-pink sea.

"Really?" She asked. "Can you at least tell me what those problems might be?"

He didn't answer and she pressed him further. "Have you ever had problems with one before?"

"Not exactly." He cut himself a brownie and bit into it. "These really are good, Zoe."

He slowly chewed and swallowed. "No," he repeated. "Not directly. But, we did have trouble with a couple of people who attended, back when I was working in South Carolina."

"It was mainly drinking and vandalism, meaning that they were drunk and smashed up a couple of the booths and damaged some merchandise."

"It was an overall pain in the backside for everyone involved. As a result, we had to be there every day, and that left us potentially short-handed for other situations that might have come up."

"So what you're telling me," she said, "is that no other situations did come up and nothing more happened, but it might have."

Hugh pressed his mouth into a thin line and Zoe reached across the table to lay her hand on his arm.

"Not to seem unsympathetic, but logically, you might have had trouble with drunks anywhere else, too. That type of situation isn't specifically limited to Renaissance Faires, is it?"

At that point, the back door slammed and the girls rushed in. They stopped when they saw the pan of brownies in front of Hugh, and Kate cut some pieces for herself and Sarah.

"Hey, we heard today that a Renaissance Faire is coming to Corolla," she said, as she filled two glasses with milk and pulled out some napkins.

"Is it true?"

"Yes, but I can't believe you've heard about it already," her mother answered.

"The decision was just made and I didn't think the news had gone public, yet."

"I heard about it from my art teacher," Sarah explained. "He said that the Faire is looking for some art students to help paint scenery and props for the plays and things."

"Wow, Sarah!" Zoe exclaimed. "Are you going to volunteer?" Sarah, whose mouth was full of chocolate, nodded.

"I am SO jealous," Kate said with a grin. "Hey, if they come up with anything that I can do too, let me know, okay?"

After the girls had thoroughly discussed the Faire and its possibilities, they scampered off upstairs.

Zoe took Hugh's hand and led him into the living room and over to the couch where they sat close together, each hoping to make peace with the other.

"I'm truly sorry that you are upset, Hugh," she said, as she smoothed the front of her sweater, "but please explain to me how dealing with trouble at the Faire is different from dealing with it anywhere else."

"I just can't shake the feeling that there is more to this than what you're telling me."

"It isn't different," he admitted. "But the people are just so…so unusual." He shrugged.

"And, it looks to me like a magnet for trouble. Do we need any more of that around here?"

Zoe looked puzzled. "It's not like Corolla is a hot-bed of crime, Hugh," she said.

"Don't you like it being quiet?" he persisted. "Not that it's terribly quiet during tourist season, as you know. But, that's the thing. The Faire will move us into tourist season earlier than usual, and then we'll have even more hassles than we normally do."

"I see your point," she said soothingly. "But look at it this way. The Faire will bring in money for two good causes and it will only last one week. That's not so bad, is it?"

Hugh shrugged. "I guess we'll just have to deal with whatever comes."

Chapter 15

Susan tightly gripped a cup of hot tea and looked at the morning sun. The dazzling brightness on the water lit the front rooms of her house where the curtains were pulled back and the windows open. However, her thoughts were far away from the water that morning.

She had not returned to her mother's house since her accident. At first, she hadn't felt up to it. Then she had to admit that she was also afraid someone sinister would be waiting for her there. Someone who wanted her dead.

She had to go back soon, though. In the meanwhile, she had been busy meeting with people to walk over her land and discuss boundaries and options, some of which required negotiations that Zoe helped settle.

There were times when she wondered if all the fuss was worth the effort. It was all so complicated and she didn't understand business, very well.

Thankfully, Zoe had taken the brunt of responsibility for most of the issues, and realistically, there was no other way to get the money that she needed.

The phone rang. "Hi Susie," Rose said. "I'm checking to see how you are, and to offer to go with you to your mother's house this morning."

"John agreed to mind the store again today. I really think he enjoys it," she said, "though he'll never admit that."

"He likes to talk almost as much as I do, and that's saying something," she laughed.

Susan thanked her, relieved that she wouldn't be going alone. "I was just thinking that I needed to go back soon, she admitted. "And you have no idea how much I dreaded it."

It was a beautiful morning, much too nice to be stuck inside. But the work had to be done, and Rose parked her car in front of the house, near the front steps.

The trees were turning a misty green color, and a northerly breeze met them as they got out of the car.

Susan thought that most of the chilliness somehow emanated from the house itself, and felt the hair on the back of her neck rise when she crossed the threshold.

Her thoughts turned to the local legend of the Ghost Horse. His story was an old one, and while it was true that he was very rarely seen, it was also a fact that he did, at times, appear when someone was in grave danger.

She wondered if he would save her from the person who wished her harm, just as he had saved Zoe, Kate, and Sarah, the year before.

Probably not. For the thousandth time, she wondered if she had simply fallen off the chair instead of being pushed. Maybe having a concussion meant that you couldn't entirely trust your memory.

Rose broke into her thoughts. "Let's get started, Susie. I have to admit that this place makes me uneasy, but I don't want you here by yourself."

"I'll help as much as I can, and so will Zoe and Hugh, whenever they are able. My point is that we'll help you get through it."

"Thank you," Susan's voice rose. "But I shouldn't need a babysitter Rose, not at my age. I have always taken care of myself and my problems. Up until now, that is," she added.

"Of course," Rose said soothing. "But this is different. We can't leave you alone here until we find out what's going on."

"Your injuries could have been a lot worse, and you could even have died. Don't you know that having you around means more to us than giving up a few hours of our time to help you?"

Susan blinked back unexpected tears and said, "I don't know what to say."

"You don't have to say anything," Rose told her. "And now, "let's finish this living room. Then, we can move to the dining room and work our way to the back of the house."

"We also need to set aside anything that might be valuable so that Zoe can look at it, later."

The two women made good progress through the downstairs front rooms that morning. All was well until about two hours later, when they heard creaking in the upstairs hallway, as well as a door closing.

In silent, mutual agreement, they tiptoed toward the front door and Susan unlocked it as quietly as possible.

She whispered, "That's the same sound I heard the night I was alone here and fell."

Rose gripped her hand and they waited, but heard nothing else. After a while, they tiptoed back into the dining room and quietly resumed with their work, stopping to listen periodically, just in case.

They agreed that neither of them wanted to venture into the back rooms that morning, and Rose suggested that they wait for Hugh and Zoe.

By noon, they were both more than ready to leave and, with great relief, Susan locked the door and suggested that they celebrate by having lunch.

They had left behind a growing pile of items that might, or might not, be of value. Zoe would make those decisions.

Rose drove them to a small diner called *Nick's*, where each ordered a tuna- melt sandwich and iced tea.

"Are you going to call Zoe about going over to look at that pile of stuff?" Rose asked, as she carefully cut her sandwich in half.

"Maybe tomorrow," Susan said. "As a matter of fact, I was just thinking that we should probably try to finish the entire downstairs before she comes."

By this time, they agreed that they had been too easily frightened and that what they'd heard was probably a mouse or some other small animal that had, somehow, made it into the house.

Rose said, "Let's just ask her to come soon. It won't matter if the entire downstairs is sorted, or not. It's not like she could get through all of it in one day, anyway."

She quietly had her doubts about the large, old-fashioned kitchen, in particular. She had poked around enough to realize that the kitchen cupboards were entirely stuffed with who-knew-what, hopefully most of which could be thrown away.

Chapter 16

By mid-May the air had grown gentle, and at times, down-right hot. Local excitement and involvement in the Renaissance Faire blossomed as prolifically as Nature's unfolding, and Hugh seemed to be the only person in Currituck County who wasn't looking forward to it.

Kate found her niche at the Faire, after all. She would help Mandy Wren look after the participating horses, though thankfully, a veterinarian was also going to be on-site for several hours each day.

In addition, they would ride through the Faire as costumed characters at times, to add to the medieval atmosphere.

Sarah was excited about selling her art and helping out. Her teacher had arranged for the class to have their own tent, and participating students were scheduled to create displays and sell merchandise.

Sarah's talent clearly lay in watercolor painting, though admittedly, she hadn't tried to work with anything else, so far.

Her paintings were delicate to the point of ethereal, and were unlike any that Zoe had seen before. When asked to describe them, she would say, "fairy-like," and wondered who Sarah had inherited her talent from.

However, Sarah's family background was likely to remain a mystery, forever. The girl was, by nature, much quieter than her sister, Kate. But her eyes shone with excitement and her smile was wide whenever the Faire was discussed—which was often—both at home and at school.

The girls impatiently felt like it would be forever until the Faire opened, though in reality, those involved had to put in a lot of work to be ready on time.

When the day finally arrived to set up, nearly everyone managed to arrive by sunrise, though some came even earlier.

The excitement was nearly tangible as people shouted greetings to one another and exchanged jokes with friends and acquaintances.

The sun was already hot, but a cool breeze blew in from the Sound that would hopefully last throughout the day.

The waves on the Sound were gentle that morning, and a lone crane flew overhead as Susan stood in the shade of the trees that surrounded her house and excitedly watched from a distance.

When Zoe and the girls were finally free to walk through the grounds, they were excited to see so many people and tents.

Renee, who was overseeing everything, waved them away when Zoe went back to ask what else was needed. So, they walked across the field to meet Susan, who had set up a card table and chairs within the shelter of the trees.

The table was covered with a clean, white cloth and was set with paper plates and cups.

As soon as she saw them, Susan carried out a carton of orange juice, a pot of hot coffee, egg-and-bacon breakfast sandwiches, and blueberry muffins. By the time they arrived there was nothing to do but sit down and eat.

They were surprised, but pleased. None of them had eaten much at home and they were starving.

They seated themselves comfortably, and ate, and talked, occasionally glancing in the direction of the Faire where a lot of laughter and shouting was going on.

"I hope this works out well," Susan said. Her attention was mostly focused on the activity instead of her guests, and Zoe reminded her that there was nothing to worry about.

Susan though, seemed resistant to Zoe's reassurances, so she finally gave up and focused on her food, instead.

Just as Kate reached for the last blueberry muffin, she abruptly stopped with her hand in the air.

"Hey, there's Mandy! I need to go see if she needs me."

"We'll all go, Kate," her mother said. "I want to see how everything is coming along anyway, and I need to check in with Renee again."

She turned to Susan. "Let's clear up here, and then you can come with us. I think you'll feel better once you see how everything looks. And, you should meet some of the people, too."

"No, not just now," Susan shook her head. "I don't need any help with these things; you all just go along and I'll come over later."

Zoe shrugged. "Well, if you're sure," she said, not wanting to nag.

On the way over, they saw Hugh and Jake striding toward Noah Brent's house. Kate asked, "Mom, what's Hugh doing over there?"

"I don't know, Kate," she said. "Maybe he's going to talk to them about Susan's accident."

"You never know, they might have seen someone hanging around her house the night that she fell. And I know he still suspects that someone pushed her off the chair."

Chapter 17

Hugh knocked, and a tall, heavy-set woman opened the sturdy, oak door so quickly that she must have been watching them as they approached. She suspiciously asked what they wanted.

"Are you Mrs. Brent?" Hugh asked. "I'm Deputy Hugh McKenzie and this is my partner, Jake Starling. We'd like to come in, if that's okay. We want to ask you and your husband a few questions."

By this time, Noah Brent had also reached the door, and he pushed past his wife to open it wider so they could enter.

"Sure," he offered a friendly grin. "We're always happy to help the police. But why us? What's up? Before we get into that, though, come on through and have a seat," he said.

"Analee will get us some coffee, won't you?"

The look Analee shot him was clearly not one of agreement, but she left and returned a few minutes later with cups, saucers, and a coffee pot. She might have been pushed into offering them coffee, but she wasn't going to supply anything else.

Noah was clearly embarrassed as she slammed the tray down onto a convenient coffee table. He gave her a pointed look and asked if they would care for anything in their coffee.

Then he asked her to bring in a plate of peanut-butter cookies that she had baked the day before, which sent her striding out of the room in a huff.

As soon as she was out of sight, Noah looked at Hugh. "Please forgive my wife's rudeness, gentlemen. She really doesn't mean anything by it. She doesn't like people to come to the house. She always thinks they're up to something."

"We do what we can to get along and lead normal lives," Noah explained, "but some days are worse than others, and this seems to be one of her worse days."

"We understand," Hugh said, and Jake nodded his agreement.

"We're sorry to have to bother you, at all." He reached for a cup and saucer. "We're here because we're investigating an incident that happened to your neighbor, Susan Hall."

Noah seemed surprised as he looked from Hugh to Jake, and back to Hugh.

"She had an accident a couple of weeks ago. Didn't you know?" Hugh asked.

"No," Noah rubbed his chin. "I didn't know anything about it."

"That's hard to imagine in a small place like this, where news usually travel with the speed of light," Hugh answered.

His grin took the sting out of his words, but Noah grasped his point and blustered.

"We don't get out much anymore, Deputy McKenzie. And when we do, we don't tend to linger long and visit with folks."

"As you can see, that's a problem for my wife. So, we buy whatever we need, and do whatever we need to do, and come home again."

Hugh was inclined to believe him. Considering Analee's social problems, they probably weren't too welcome to linger anyplace, anyway.

In spite of Hugh's hard questions, Noah repeatedly swore that neither of them knew anything that might be helpful. They had not seen anyone suspicious on either their property or Susan's.

"And, he added, "believe me, if Analee had seen anyone like that, I'd have heard about it right away."

Hugh found no obvious reason to disbelieve him, and doubted that he was involved.

However, he did doubt Noah's sworn ignorance about the event itself, and he wondered if Analee had been the perpetrator.

She seemed unbalanced enough, and it would certainly explain Noah's silence. He would, no doubt, lie to protect her.

"You understand that we're here because we believe that someone might have actually been in her house and pushed her off a chair?" Hugh explained.

"Yes, I gathered that." Noah suddenly seemed very tired. He randomly ran his hand through his white hair and looked away from them.

"It's a terrible thing to not be safe in your own home," he said. "But I don't know what else to tell you."

"I haven't seen any strangers or anyone else around here who shouldn't have been."

"I'm sure you know that Susan's family made some enemies over the years, and you've probably also heard that my own family stopped having anything to do with them back when we were kids," he explained.

"Is that what you really want to know? If I'm getting my revenge on her?" he defiantly asked.

"It did cross my mind," Hugh admitted. "Please understand that I have to look at every possibility. I know that the Wellfords had a lot of enemies, so I figured that, at the least, you might know someone who still holds a grudge. Maybe someone who decided to get even by hurting or even killing her."

Noah protested. "Look, Deputy, we live a quiet life here."

He looked around at the darkened room. The curtains were pulled shut and an unlit fireplace flanked by bookshelves filled one wall.

The furniture was shabby, though plainly expensive, and the hardwood floor was covered with an oriental rug woven in bright shades of red, blue, and gold.

The rug provided the only color in the room. Everything else, even the paintings on the walls, was dark and muted.

Hugh wondered if Analee had chosen them. It would be fitting, if she had. She had disappeared, and he wondered if she was in the next room listening to them.

"We have nothing much to do with anyone," Noah repeated. "So if someone was out to get Susan, I would hardly be the person to know about it."

Hugh abruptly sat his cup down on its saucer and stood up. "This is good coffee. Thank you." Noah absently nodded, and Hugh knew there was no point in pushing him further.

"We might need to ask you a few more questions later, but that's all for now. Thanks for your cooperation."

He extended his hand, which Noah grasped in relief. He attempted a polite smile, but his expression was strained.

Once the two men were away from the house, Hugh said, "Before we go any farther, I need to know what you picked up on, back there."

He stopped under a shade tree and nodded in the direction of Noah's house.

Jake glanced back. "I wonder about his wife."

"When you asked him if he knew anyone who might want to harm Susan, he looked uneasy."

"I'm not saying that he did anything to her himself, but I can't help but wonder if he knows about it, all the same."

"Yeah, me too," Hugh said. "He looked more scared, the longer we were there. We'd better keep half-an-eye on both of them."

"That shouldn't be too hard to do since we'll be spending a lot of time here at the Faire." He glanced over in that direction and sighed.

"The other thing to consider besides a motive is the timing. Why now? If anyone had a grudge against Susan, why wait until now to get revenge?"

He fixed his eyes on the crowds of people who rushed back and forth, and felt his stomach clench. Was she here? And what would he do if she was?

Chapter 18

The chaos and laughter at the Renaissance Faire grew louder as the vendors and actors unpacked their belongings and set up their booths, tents, theatres.

The excitement was contagious and Zoe noticed that early-on, Kate, in particular, seemed to have a permanent grin on her face as she looked around.

"Oh Mom, this is going to be so great!" she bubbled.

"I can't wait to see where Mandy and I will be; hopefully in the middle of everything!"

"I'm pretty sure that the horses will be kept in a quieter part of the grounds, Kate," she answered.

"But that doesn't mean that you'll miss anything. You won't be on-duty all the time, and you'll also be on horse-back with a good view of everything going on.

"Will I need to stay in costume all the time?" she hopefully asked.

"Not when you're mucking out stalls, my dear," her mother chuckled. Kate's face immediately fell, and her mother added, "But you will definitely be in costume when you're part of the scenery here—riding through the faire and so-forth."

"So, what we need to do first is to find suitable costumes for both you and Sarah."

With Kate's excited grin restored, Zoe turned to Sarah, whose attention had wandered. She was staring at an unusually tall man who stood quietly at the edge of the field with his arms crossed.

He, in turn, was watching the activity unfolding before him. Zoe wondered if he was a tourist, and why Sarah found him so interesting.

Just then, a short, burly man with a light-brown beard called to the man. "Hey, Friend, can you lend us a hand over here?"

The tall man shot him a good natured grin and hurried over to where the burly man struggled with a corner of a huge tent.

The problem was the wind. It was growing stronger and whipping the canvas out of his hands before he could fasten it down.

Zoe and the girls watched for a few minutes and then moved away to go look for costumes.

"Will you have one too, Mom?" Kate asked. "You really should, you know. It would be fun for all of us, and we could have our pictures taken together."

Zoe agreed that if she saw a costume she couldn't resist, she would buy it. The girls eagerly offered to help her pick one out, which made her smile.

As they walked, Sarah confided, "I'm a little scared about working here. I'm not very comfortable around people, anyway.

The teacher has us scheduled to work with partners but what if someone, a customer, gives us a hard time? What would I do?"

"That's nothing to be afraid of, Child," a strange, lilting voice answered from behind them. It was the tall man whom Sarah had been watching earlier. He approached them with a gentle smile on his face.

At first glance, he appeared to be a young man. But Zoe soon saw that his face was creased from the sun and his brilliant, blue eyes were not those of a young man.

Wind ruffled his longish, gold hair, and he held what appeared to be a cup of tea in one hand.

"I don't mean to intrude," he apologized. "I only meant that everyone at the Faire watches out for each another. I can promise that no one will bother your daughter and get away with it."

Instinctively, to her surprise, Zoe immediately liked him.

"I'm not sure why," she hesitated, "but I almost believe you. Except that I don't know why I should." Amusement flickered in his eyes.

Who are you?" she asked in a friendly voice. "And what do you do here?" Her gesture encompassed their surroundings.

"I do anything that needs to be done," his smile grew. "But, I don't sell things, if that's what you mean. And, I'm only here to help out."

"Sometimes there are problems with the animals or structures, and sometimes people who work here just need to take a break. So, I help wherever I can."

"My name is Aengus," he introduced himself, "though you might have heard Harvey over there," he pointed at a thin, wiry man to their right who was broadly gesturing, "shouting it a few minutes ago." They shook their heads.

"No? Well anyway, it is an appropriate name for someone who helps at a Renaissance Faire, don't you think?"

Zoe returned his smile. "Yes it is, now that you mention it."

"I'm Zoe, and these are my daughters, Sarah and Kate." She nodded at each of them and Aengus solemnly shook their hands.

Kate met his eyes with an open, friendly grin, but Sarah looked puzzled and frowned slightly as she looked into his eyes.

"No doubt we will be seeing a lot of each other this week," he said, and gently touched Sarah's shoulder.

What more might have been said was interrupted by the approach of Hugh and Jake. Hugh's eyes swept over them, then focused on Aengus.

Zoe introduced the three men and shot a warning look at Hugh. But his eyes remained on Aengus and they politely nodded at one another.

Clearly sensing tension, Aengus excused himself. "I see that Harvey is once again in need of help."

He nodded in the direction of the man who was still persistently waving.

Zoe waited until he'd left before she looked at Hugh and asked, "What's wrong? Why were you rude to that man?"

"It's not just him," he snapped. "The truth is, I don't want any of this crew to be here at all. And that's a good enough reason."

The girls looked away in embarrassment, as did Jake. None of them had seen Hugh and Zoe angry at each another, and it was something of a shock.

Hugh was typically so easy-going that people tended to forget that he might also have a temper.

Jake feigned a sudden interest in one of the booths nearby, and wandered over to take a closer look.

"If you don't like what's going on," Zoe spoke between clenched teeth, "then I strongly suggest that you go find *other* people to be angry with. Maybe someone who actually deserves it." Her green eyes flashed fire.

"Zoe…" he met her eyes, then looked down and nudged the soft earth with the toe of his boot.

"I don't want to fight with you. But this whole thing just puts me on edge." He gestured at the activity around them.

"I don't understand that," she answered, "because you haven't given me a good reason to do so."

"You know," she moved closer and looked searchingly at him, "I can't help but take this personally because I'm the one who encouraged Renee to go ahead with this plan and to involve Susan, too."

"I thought that you would at least be supportive of it for those reasons."

Hugh changed his mind about whatever he had been about to say, and turned away.

"Come on, Jake," he called. "Let's take a walk through this place and let everyone know that we're around. We need to establish our presence, here."

Jake flashed an uneasy look at Zoe, and hurried to catch up with him. The girls' eyes were wide as they looked from their mother to Hugh.

"It's okay," Zoe reassured them. "He'll calm down and everything will be fine. Meanwhile, we have some dresses to buy."

As they turned to go, Sarah violently tugged at Zoe's sleeve and she looked around in time to see a tall, slim woman scream and hurl herself directly at Hugh.

The woman was dressed in a leather jacket, blue-jeans, and high heels. Her hair was long and dark, and from what they could see of her, she was beautiful.

Hugh reflexively caught her in his arms and she clung to him a moment before kissing him fully on the mouth.

Instinctively, Hugh and Jake looked back at Zoe with expressions of shock on their faces, even as Hugh kept an arm around the unknown woman.

As one, the girls and their mother turned and walked away. They didn't see the dark-haired woman flash a brilliant, and perhaps triumphant, smile in their direction.

Meanwhile, standing apart with his arms crossed, Aengus watched with a thoughtful, yet grim, expression on his face. "The fool," he uttered.

But which "fool" he referred to, was unclear.

Chapter 19

As usual, Hugh stopped at Zoe's house on his way home from work that evening. He was unsure of his welcome, but he needed to talk to her.

Zoe was in the kitchen stirring something on the stove while the girls sat at the table working on one of Sarah's art projects. She had decided to try her hand at jewelry-making to sell at the Faire, along with her watercolors.

They acted as though they hadn't heard him come in, and perhaps they hadn't, though he had his doubts.

Even Woolf didn't greet him as he normally did, but kept his place on the floor between the stove and the table, instead.

When Hugh walked in, the German shepherd raised his head and uttered a quiet "Woof" of welcome. Or maybe it was a warning; he couldn't be sure.

Could a dog understand such things as inner human conflict? In Woolf's case, he thought there was a good possibility.

Hugh watched the little family diligently ignore him, and was half-tempted to leave.

But in his quiet way, he could be just as stubborn as Zoe. And besides, he did owe her an explanation and was afraid to leave it too long.

"Zoe," he said. She turned and met his eyes, then grabbed a dish towel, wiped her hands on it, and tossed it on the counter.

Without directly looking at either of them, the girls hurriedly gathered their things up and headed for the stairs.

"I need to talk to you, Zoe," he insisted.

Grim-faced, she pushed past him and led the way into the living room where she perched on the edge of a chair and waited. It was not a good sign.

He sat down opposite her, on the edge of the couch, trying to gauge her level of receptiveness. But he was afraid that she had already shut him out.

She cleared her throat and tapped one foot impatiently. That was not a good sign, either.

"I'm waiting," was all she said. He took a deep breath and hoped for the best.

"Okay. You know as well as I do, that there's still a lot about each other that we don't know. And, this is one of those examples." He made an effort to sound matter-of-fact.

She nodded. "Go on."

"Well, we've both been in other relationships over the years. I mean," he spoke more quickly, "that neither of us is exactly a kid anymore, are we?"

"So we both have had relationships with other people." She stared at him.

"What I mean to say is," he tried again, "is that the woman who kissed me at the Faire is someone I knew years ago and, to tell you the truth, I was once engaged to her. Her name is Maggie," he added.

"So," Zoe said, "when, exactly, did you break off your engagement to Maggie?" She sat up straighter.

"To tell you the truth," he admitted, "I never did formally break it off."

Her eyebrows shot up and she opened her mouth, but he interrupted her.

112

"You need to understand that this was maybe seven or eight years ago. She was working for herself at the time, selling gravestone rubbings at Renaissance Faires and other kinds of festivals."

"She came to where I was living at the time, to see what she could find in the old church cemeteries in that place. That's how we met."

"In the end, we just drifted apart and lost touch with each other. We went our separate ways," he explained.

"That's why I didn't want the Faire to come here," he told her. "I thought there was a chance that she might still be traveling with them, and I knew how involved you and the girls were going to be."

"I also knew that if Maggie came, you would certainly find out about her because she isn't one to go away gently."

Zoe examined her hands. "Are you planning to formally break off your engagement to her, now that she's here? Or, do you plan to resume it?"

"Of course, I intend to break off with her," he was close to shouting. "But I couldn't do it yesterday on the spur of the moment."

"I'm sure she considers our relationship over with, too. I mean, we haven't been in touch in all this time, so what else could she think?"

"I suppose that depends on her expectations, Hugh. Meanwhile, I strongly suggest that you straighten this out. Otherwise, you have no way of actually knowing what she's thinking."

"I will, Honey," he gave her an earnest look. "In fact, I'm going to meet up with her for dinner this evening, and I promise to set her straight, then."

Zoe's lips tightened. "Before you do that, you'd better consider what you really want, Hugh."

"Do you really *want* to break it off with Maggie? You need to know beyond the shadow of a doubt." Her throat constricted. "But this needs to be resolved, now."

He nodded and stood up. "Okay. I'll take care of it. You do believe that you're the one I really want, don't you?"

She shrugged. "Talk to Maggie, and decide if that's true or not."

Without another word, he picked up his hat and quietly closed the door behind himself.

Chapter 20

After Zoe and the others walked away, Aengus stood quietly and considered what he had just seen.

It was none of his business, he was well-aware of that, but it was hard not to care when he saw danger clearly approaching good people.

He had always been like that; it was in his nature and he had learned over the years, and through much living, to accept who he was.

Gradually, he resumed his walk through the Faire, stopping to chat with people and looking at what they were selling. He would take in a couple of the performances later that evening.

When he reached the border where the field began, he saw Susan in the distance, folding up her table and chairs.

He strode out toward her and as he drew closer, began to whistle so that she would hear him and hopefully, look up. She did.

With his hands disarmingly shoved into his pockets, he smiled at her. But as he approached, his attention was drawn away from her and to the house itself, and then to the Sound where the small waves lapped the shore, and lastly, to the neighbor's house in the distance.

It was an idyllic setting, but something was clearly wrong here, too.

"I don't mean to interfere with your work," he called to her, "but I did want to introduce myself since you live in this beautiful place by the sea and close to the Faire."

Susan was as disarmed by his lilting voice and his smile as Zoe had been. She felt as though she was greeting an old friend instead of a man whom she had never seen before.

Aengus pointed at the house in the distance and asked, "Who lives there?"

"Oh," she said, "the Brents. We've been neighbors nearly forever since the two houses were built, though theirs is a little younger than my own. I don't live here," she continued, then realized her blunder.

She hadn't intended for anyone to know that the house was not occupied.

"But while the Faire is here, I will be staying here, as well," she fibbed.

Aengus recognized the lie for what it was. He'd seen her expression change the moment she'd admitted that the house was unoccupied, and he felt sorry for her. He could see that she wore her burdens heavily.

"No need to worry," he gently reassured her. "I have no wish to either rob your house or to disturb your peace."

She looked at him in surprise, then murmured, "Thank you."

Then she further surprised herself by asking, "Would you like to sit down for a while?"

She unfolded two of the chairs again, and they sat in the shade of the trees.

"Are you enjoying all this?" he gestured toward the activity across the field.

"I don't know, yet," she confided. She went on to explain how Zoe had arranged everything, and Aengus listened so intently, his eyes never leaving hers, that she found herself also confessing her need for money and her concerns about what to do with the house.

In the end, she realized that she had told him everything, even about the questionable history of her ancestors.

She found herself to be both relieved and appalled, and also, suddenly, very tired.

Aengus saw it, and offered to make her a cup of tea. She readily agreed, and led the way to the kitchen without apologizing for the surrounding clutter.

Strangely, because she hadn't remembered they existed, she opened a cupboard door and pulled out the egg-shell-delicate, Limoge china cups and saucers that had been her grandmother's.

She carefully washed and dried these while Aengus made the tea much stronger than she was used to drinking.

Long afterwards, she could never explain to herself what had possessed her to find and use that china.

Aengus, who seemed to find nothing strange about sipping tea out of delicate, antique cups, said, "Now tell me about your neighbors, the Brents. What are they like?"

"Oh, we were out of touch with each other for years. And then somehow, we became reacquainted again."

"I knew Noah as a boy, but our families took a dislike to each other when we were young, so we never had a chance to play together, much."

"That is a shame," he murmured, his voice as soft as the sea. "There is so much more to focus on in life than counting the heads of your enemies. And all the time wondering how to cheat them."

Susan caught her breath. How could he possibly know that her family had spent much of their time reciting the sins of their enemies and wondering how best to make them pay.

She found Aengus to be a little frightening, but he was also comforting and safe. That wasn't rational, but it was the only way to describe her feelings.

She considered herself broad-minded regarding anything mystical, but this man was something new.

He wasn't what she would call "safe," but at the same time, she knew that he was the safest thing under the sun.

Eventually, she realized that he was asking her where she lived.

"My house is on the beach where there are no roads. Where the wild horses are," she told him.

"Wild horses!" he carefully sat his cup and saucer down on the table. "Tell me about them."

"They've been here since the 1500s," she proudly explained. "They're descendants of the Spanish mustangs that came over on their ships.

What with ship-wrecks and the need to reduce their weight when they got stuck on hidden sand bars, the horses either swam ashore or were purposely left behind. They have survived here ever since."

"It's harder for them now, though," she added. "All the development, you know."

"Ah, that's the thing, isn't it?" he slowly stood up. "Everything in this world would survive and thrive in balance if it wasn't for humans."

"Yes," she agreed, and then felt strongly compelled to add, "You're very welcome to visit me there sometime, too. We could walk the shore and look for the horses."

"I'll do that, Susan," he agreed. "I'll do that very soon." He pointed at the Sound. "Do you ever see swans, here?"

"Yes." His question surprised her. "They tend to migrate here in the fall. Quite a lot of them, and they're hunted."

He looked out over the water. "I'm very, very sorry to hear that."

"And now, "he reached for his jacket, "try not to worry anymore. I'm sure that all will come right, in the end."

Susan watched him walk away. What was it about him? He compelled her to be more honest than she wanted to be—perhaps more honest than it was good for anyone to be. Yes, that was it, she decided.

She was always relieved to reach the sand where the paved road ended.

This was her home, she told herself. This place was in her blood—not that other place on Currituck Sound where she had grown up.

Here was the freedom; the relative quiet; the endless restlessness of the ocean; the wild horses. These were her home.

That night, she slept more peacefully than she had done in a very long time. But sometime in the night she turned over, awakened by the soft whinnying of a horse beneath her window.

She hurriedly got up and looked, but did not see a horse.

The clouds raced across the nearly-full moon as it whispered shafts of light onto the shore. She looked toward the sea and wondered what time it was.

A cloud suddenly shifted and she clearly saw a figure near the shore. Right beside it stood a white horse. *The* white horse—the Ghost Horse. She was sure of it.

She caught her breath and strained to look more closely. But at that moment a cloud scudded over the moon. She waited until it passed and when she could see again, the figure and the horse were both gone.

Chapter 21

Hugh didn't call the next morning, and the girls anxiously watched Zoe while they packed their things for the Renaissance Faire that afternoon.

They tried to be subtle, which resulted in their not being very subtle at all. But the worried expressions on their faces mirrored that of her own, and she couldn't help but wonder if Hugh and Maggie had done more than have dinner the night before. Maybe Maggie was his choice, after all.

They were nearly ready to leave when Zoe's cell phone rang, and it was Hugh, after all.

"Hi, Honey," his voice was hesitant. "Just thought I'd check in with you and wish you a good day."

"Thanks," she said. "We're leaving shortly, but I have a few minutes to talk."

He said, "Okay," but didn't offer anything more.

Finally, she took a deep breath to steady herself and asked, "Did you get everything straightened out with Maggie, last night?"

"Not exactly," he answered. "Look, Zoe, this is more complicated than I had hoped it would be."

"I'm going to take care of everything, but it's going to take a little longer than I'd planned, and I need you to be patient with me."

"Is that because you're not sure which of us you really want?" she bluntly asked.

"*Please*, Honey," he sounded shocked. "It's not like that. I can't exactly explain. I made a promise... you're just going to have to trust me on this."

"Hugh…," she began, but he interrupted her. "Please, Zoe. It's not what you think, but I can't explain right now."

"I may not be able to see you much for the next few days, but nothing has changed between us. Okay?"

"Hugh, can you promise me that you're not trying to court us both because you can't make a clear decision?"

He sighed. "I can honestly promise you that, but it's up to you whether you choose to believe me."

"I'm just asking you to trust me. Is it really that hard for you to do?"

"I don't know," she answered, and hung up.

The girls were hovering nearby as Zoe gathered up her things, and picked up Woolf's leash.

"Come along, boy. You're the only reliable man in my life." She gently stroked his face as he anxiously looked up at her.

"I want you with us this afternoon," she explained as she leaned over and kissed the top of his head.

Once the girls had settled themselves in the Jeep, she handed them drinks and snacks.

She didn't have much to do at the Faire, but she didn't like the idea of leaving the girls alone there, in spite of what Aengus said about everyone looking out for everyone else.

As usual, Zoe parked near Susan's house. And as soon as Kate spotted Mandy with the horses, she took off running.

"Kate!" Her mother shouted. "You've forgotten your costume!" Kate ran back to retrieve it.

She didn't actually need it until later, but Mandy had wanted them to practice riding in their costumes first, just in case adjustments needed to be made for the sake of comfort, and possibly, modesty.

Mandy waved and smiled, and Zoe and Sarah waved back before heading over to the school's art tent where they found Mr. Murray, the teacher, tensely pacing and shouting into his cell phone.

When he saw them, he stuffed the phone back into his pocket and lowered his voice.

"I can't believe this!" He waved his clenched fists at the sky. "Our very first day and Robert Merriweather won't be here, after all."

"I must have two people working together. After all, there are liability issues."

"What happened?" Zoe asked. She glanced at Sarah who looked decidedly scared, and added, "I'm sure we can sort this out, whatever it is."

"Robert was playing football with some other kids and managed to crack a rib. The problem is that I can't stay here today, and I can't find anyone else who can come on such short notice."

"The folks who are scheduled to work later will be on time, but my problem is what to do about it right now."

"I can stay for a while," Zoe told him. "After all, things happen and I'm sure that someone, or maybe several people, will be willing to fill in for him for the rest of the week if he can't make it."

"Cracked ribs are very painful, you know. I'm sure that he's no happier about it than you are," she added.

In a calmer voice, Mr. Murray assured her that he was upset for Sarah's sake. "I'll be available too, but just not at the moment," he explained. "In fact, not at all today."

He left them and hurried away muttering about people who make commitments and don't keep them.

"Wow, Mom," Sarah said. "I've never seen him like that. I really don't think Robert hurt himself on purpose."

She looked worried as she sat down beside a table laden with displays of jewelry. "Why is Mr. Murray blaming him for hurting himself? Anyone can have an accident."

"I know, Sarah," she answered. "It isn't sensible to think otherwise."

"But Mr. Murray wants everything to go well. He'll calm down, my dear. Please don't worry about it."

"Meanwhile," she looked around, "we'll be fine. We can take turns having breaks when we need to, because Woolf is with us and you know he'll take care of us. Are you okay with that?"

Sarah nodded, though she was obviously still upset by her art teacher's tirade.

"Yes. As long as Woolf is here with us, we'll be fine. And Mom," she added, "that tall man we met yesterday said that people here look out for each other, too."

Zoe tightened her lips. "I remember, Sarah, and I'm sure he means well. But I tend to put a lot more faith in Woolf than in the words of someone I don't know. Meanwhile, let's get some of this other stuff put up."

"Would you grab a few of those paintings? We'll hang them on this lattice—it looks sturdy enough to support them, and I see the hooks in a box right over there." She pointed at a large box that sat on the ground behind the table.

They also managed to arrange the jewelry, some hand-died scarves, and small sculptures, before the crowd picked up.

An hour later, they were so busy that there was no time to think of anything except selling and wrapping merchandise. Fortunately, Sarah was kept too busy to feel either shy or scared.

After a while, when the crowd finally diminished somewhat, Zoe felt she could safely leave Sarah to go check on Kate.

She also needed to find Renee to make sure that all was running smoothly, and to explain about having to stay with Sarah.

"I'll be as quick as I can," she said to her daughter. "You have your cell phone with you, and I want you to call me if you need me. Okay?"

"I will, Mom, and everything will be fine," Sarah answered. To Zoe's relief, the girl was clearly feeling more confident than she had been earlier.

In fact, Sarah handled the crowd of shoppers very well. She seemed to enjoy answering questions and helping people make their choices.

Even more surprising was the fact that she seemed to have quite a knack for it. People responded to her gentle manner, and they liked her. It was easy to see that.

As she briskly strode through the Faire, Zoe glimpsed Hugh in the distance in his uniform, striding through the crowd as though he was in a hurry.

He didn't see her, and she wondered if they would meet. But then he moved away, and for a moment she could hardly breathe. She wondered if that was symbolic. Maybe he was moving away from her in every way.

"Don't be silly," she told herself. Then again, this was the man who had never broken off his engagement to a woman he hadn't seen in years, and had meanwhile sworn his love to her and wanted to marry her. What kind of a person did that?

Deep down, she wanted to believe that he loved her. But what if he didn't love her enough?

"I hope I have not been a fool," she told herself.

Chapter 22

Once she had seen that all was well with Kate, Zoe caught up with Renee who was working at her laptop computer in a small building resembling a medieval garden shed. "How are you holding up?" she asked.

Renee ran a hand through her hair and grinned at her. "About what you'd imagine."

"What a lot of work! On the other hand, we have quite a crowd and that's terrific. We can rest next week when it's over with."

"By then, we may both need a vacation," Zoe agreed. "I just hope that it continues to be this popular all week." She explained about Sarah's situation.

"Everything is fine," Renee told her, "and there's really nothing for you to do right now, anyway. Go on and help your daughter today."

"Let's check in with each other this evening. Maybe we can grab some dinner around 5:30. Will that work for you?"

"That would be great," Zoe told her. By that time, other students would have taken charge of the art tent and they would all be free.

She was on her way back to Sarah when she heard a commotion that included people shouting and a dog barking. She instantly recognized Woolf's bark and broke into a run.

She pushed her way through the crowd that had slowed down to look at whatever was happening.

Once, she badly stumbled over uneven ground and nearly fell. But she quickly righted herself and saw Hugh directly in front of her, running as fast as he could, shouting, "Get out of the way!"

A large crowd was gathered in front of the art tent. Woolf, with hackles raised, paced in front of Sarah, growling and snarling with his teeth bared and his ears flat.

Aengus and another man were holding a third man by the arms, who was struggling to free himself while shouting for help.

"Thank God!" he bellowed when he saw Hugh. "You need to arrest these idiots! And that dog," he pointed at Woolf, "needs to be put down!"

Without asking what happened, Hugh pulled the man's arms behind his back and hand-cuffed him.

"I know that dog, Mister," he said between clenched teeth, "and he wouldn't be threatening you unless you'd done something to deserve it. You'd better be thankful that he didn't get to you before these men did."

Hugh straightened up. "Now," he turned to Aengus, "what happened?"

Before Aengus could answer, Hugh turned to the crowd and shouted, "Okay, everyone, just go about your business."

"Everything is fine here. We appreciate your help. Just go on now, and have a good time."

He waited until the crowd reluctantly drifted away, thanks to additional encouragement from Jake, who arrived shortly behind Hugh and Zoe.

Once everyone had moved away, Aengus introduced the other man who had helped, as Arthur Lake. Aengus nodded at Sarah.

"Do you want to tell him?" he asked. She nodded and seemed to Hugh to be remarkably calm, considering the commotion.

Zoe was at her side, petting Woolf and softly talking to him, to calm him. She put her other arm around Sarah and pulled her close.

Hugh looked inquiringly at Sarah, who angrily pointed. "He tried to steal a necklace. I saw him do it. But he laughed and told me that there was nothing that a little girl like me could do to stop him."

"He didn't see Woolf lying on the other side of the table, though. And Woolf went after him."

"Honestly, Mom," she turned to Zoe with shining eyes, "you should have seen Woolf. He leaped right over the table and grabbed that man by the seat of his pants."

"He tried to run, but he was too slow and Woolf grabbed him," Sarah giggled. "It was the most wonderful thing I've ever seen."

"Then," she continued, "Aengus and Arthur got here and I told Woolf it was okay to let go."

"He did, but I think it was only because they were here. He likes Aengus," she added.

Hugh looked at the would-be thief. "Do we need an ambulance?" He motioned to Jake.

"Go ahead and call one. We'll have him checked out and then we'll arrest him."

"Not on your life!" the man shouted. "I'm not going to have people laughing at me for being bit in the butt by a vicious dog!"

Everyone broke into laughter, even the deputies. They couldn't help themselves. That made the man angrier, and he scowled at Zoe.

"I'm going to sue *you*, lady, for everything you've got." He spat at her feet.

In a split-second, Hugh had him by the front of the shirt and had nearly lifted him off the ground. "You pull a stunt like that again, Ivan, and you'll be real sorry."

"And by the way, you won't be suing anyone and let me tell you why. But first, we're going to call an ambulance, and it's just too bad about where you got bit."

"Second," he continued when the call had been made, "let me tell you now, that if you make a move to sue these people, I will charge you with the attempted assault and kidnapping of a young girl."

"And, let me also tell you that if that happens, things will not go well for you. Folks around here don't like it when kids are threatened or assaulted, and you won't have a chance in hell of not going to jail for a very long time."

The man scowled, but shut his mouth. Hugh turned to Sarah. "Are you okay, Honey? Did he hurt you or try to grab you?"

"He grabbed my arm," she answered, "but that's when Woolf went for him."

"I'm so glad Woolf was here," she confided. "I don't ever want to come here without him." She looked up at her mother.

"I promise that he will come with you whenever you're scheduled to work here, Sarah," Zoe said. "And I'll stay too, if you'd like."

"No, really," Sarah shook her head. "I'm okay as long as I have Woolf with me."

Hugh nodded. "Right. I'll need to get a statement from you in a few minutes, Sarah. And you, too," he nodded at her two rescuers."

"It's a good thing you were nearby and I really want to thank you. We'll be back shortly."

The two deputies escorted the man whom Hugh had called Ivan, back through the Faire and out to the road where the ambulance waited.

Zoe found herself more than a little disappointed that it was only Jake who returned to take their statements.

Hugh hadn't spoken to her at all, and she wondered what it meant. But then, there hadn't been much of an opportunity for a conversation, and maybe she was analyzing everything too much.

It suddenly occurred to her that Hugh knew the thief's name. He had called the man "Ivan." Maybe he had heard someone else call him by name, earlier.

Later that evening, she and the girls, along with Rose, Susan, and Renee, met up at a local café called *The Fisherman's Rest*. It was a cozy, family-owned place that was especially popular with the locals.

Sarah seemed to have fully recovered from her experience, not that she'd been terribly upset, anyway.

Zoe looked around the table at her friends and thought how very lucky she was to have them in her life.

A cool wind suddenly blew across the room as two more people hurried inside. It was Hugh, and he was with Maggie. His arm was around her, and he was gently urging her forward as she tossed her dark hair and smiled up at him. Suddenly, the room grew quiet.

Susan was the first to speak. "Come on, everyone, it's time we called it a night."

She stood up. Hugh glanced over as the others scooted their chairs back, and he saw Zoe.

His eyes held hers for a moment and then the small group of women, led by Rose, who was tightly gripping Zoe's hand, swept past him with their noses in the air. They neither looked at him nor spoke to him.

Chapter 23

That night, Zoe dreamed that she was lost in the dark somewhere near the shore. She could hear, and feel, the thunder of the sweeping tide, but she didn't call out for help because somehow, she knew that no one would hear her if she did.

She was terrified to move, afraid of being swept out into the invisible waves, and so she painfully crept along the shore.

But all at once, in the midst of the blinding darkness, she saw a white horse moving toward her and recognized him—he was the Ghost Horse.

He was still far away and she tried to call out to him. But as is usual in dreams, she was unable to make even the slightest sound, no matter how hard she tried.

The next moment, she was awake and panting with fright, the nerves in her body tingling with fearful intensity.

It was 4 a.m. but she didn't want to go back to sleep and risk falling back into the same dream. Seeing the horse should have been comforting, but it wasn't, and that worried her.

At 5:30, knowing that Susan would be awake, she telephoned and asked if they could meet at the shore and take a walk. For some reason, the fear she'd felt in the dream had grown. What if it had something to do with losing Hugh?

Without him, she would be alone in the dark. But then she told herself that was silly. She had her girls and her friends, and she certainly wasn't alone.

Maybe taking an early-morning walk would help. She always felt better when she was close to the sea.

By daybreak, Zoe and Susan were watching ghost crabs scramble back to their sandy homes to hide from scavenging birds.

The night mist thinned as the golden light of the rising sun touched the water, and it was then that Susan brought up the incident with Hugh from the previous night.

Zoe knew that she would, and dreaded it. But she hadn't wanted to be alone. The chilling fear she'd felt in the dream still clung to her like icy fingers on bare flesh.

"So, what exactly is going on with Hugh and that woman?" Susan bluntly asked.

"Her name is Maggie," Zoe answered. "Hugh was engaged to her a few years back and apparently never broke off the engagement."

"He says he's trying to sort it out, but I honestly don't know what's going on between them."

"Well of all the..." Susan groped for the right word, "stupid...things to do. How can you not break off an engagement if that's what you intend to do?" Zoe shrugged.

"Look, Honey, if I know anything, it's that Hugh loves you. Honestly, leave it to a man." She shook her head in disgust.

"I don't know how it's going to turn out, Susan, but I do know that if he can't give up Maggie, then it's really good that I'm finding out now."

Susan's lips tightened. She opened her mouth to say something, and changed her mind. Zoe took the opportunity to change the subject.

"I'll either go to your mother's house later this morning or early this afternoon," Zoe told her. "We aren't due at the Faire until around 3:00 today."

"You don't have to come with me; just let me borrow your key and I'll let you know what I find."

"By the way, if Renee is free, is it okay if she comes with me? She has some expertise in antique silver and I noticed that you had some interesting pieces. I'd like to get her opinion on those."

"Of course," Susan agreed. "I don't mind at all, and I'll keep working on things here. I'm clearing out closets and other clutter to make room for some of my mother's stuff."

"Does that mean that you're definitely not going to live in your mother's house?" Zoe turned away from the brightening sky to look at Susan.

"Yes," she admitted. "I just don't think I can face it. But if we clear everything out and fix it up, I can do something else with it."

At that moment, they turned their attention to seven or eight pelicans flying in a single-file formation over the water. They gracefully swooped into the waves, wheeling and turning as though their movements were choreographed.

"I'll never get over how amazing it is here," Zoe said. She glanced at the climbing sun. "We should turn back."

Susan agreed. "I grew up here. But each day is new and I want you to remember that, Zoe."

"I know this isn't any of my business, but please don't give up on Hugh, just yet. I've known him long enough to know that he's a good, honorable man. He wouldn't lie to you; he wouldn't tell you he loved you if he didn't. Nor would he say that he was going to break off his relationship with Maggie unless he meant it."

"I don't know, Susan," Zoe pulled her sweater tightly around herself. "I'll give it until the Faire leaves."

135

"But truthfully, this incident has made me realize how little we really know each other. And you saw them last night, the way that woman clung to him."

"That doesn't mean that *he* was clinging to *her*, Zoe. And sometimes things aren't what they appear to be."

"The truth is," Zoe said, "that he's already had a few days to break up with her, if he really wanted to do that."

Her stomach clenched, but she ignored it and abruptly asked, "Would you like to come in? I promised to take the girls to the Lighthouse this morning, but they won't be ready yet, and nothing will be open for a while, either."

"Next Saturday is when Sarah's art class will be selling their things at the Lighthouse Shop. They will be in both places, at the Faire as well as at the Lighthouse."

"Where will Sarah be?" Susan asked.

"At the Faire to begin with, until 1:00 or so. Then, I'll take her to the Lighthouse Shop for the rest of the day."

"Kate will stay at the Faire all day, but Mandy keeps a good eye on her."

"I still need to get over there and see what they have; maybe I'll do that later today," Susan said.

"I'm going to head home instead of coming over this morning. I still have so much to do." She gave Zoe a quick hug and headed toward her house.

Chapter 24

A couple of hours later, Zoe pulled into the Currituck Lighthouse parking lot. She fastened Woolf's leash onto his harness.

By the time she looked around for the girls, they were already well ahead of her.

The red-brick lighthouse dated from 1875, and the girls had been to the top several times. That didn't stop them from wanting to do it again, though.

Their last climb had been in the winter and now that it was spring, they wanted a bird's-eye-view of the world around them, and of course, the sea.

Zoe paid for their admission, and after they had stood and looked in all directions for as long as they wanted, they descended and walked over to the Lighthouse Gift Shop.

Sarah was one of Mr. Murray's better students, which was why she was going to be included in selling her things there.

Between the Renaissance Faire and the Gift Shop event, Sarah was working hard, but was happier than Zoe had ever seen her before.

Sarah had once admitted that she was afraid that nothing good would ever happen for her. But now, she was safe with Zoe and Kate.

And as a person and an artist, she was valued and respected, and most of all, loved. Even by Woolf, whom she'd been afraid of when she first met him.

Zoe asked the Shop manager where the students would be located, and she cheerfully led them back outside. They faced the charming, Victorian building and, with both hands, she pointed to either side of it.

"The tables will be on either side, and we'll put them under tents just in case it rains," she told them.

"That way, everyone will easily see all the tables. We're expecting a lot of interest and a lot of people," she smiled.

Truthfully, Mr. Murray had already explained everything his students needed to know about setting up, but Sarah had wanted to see it first-hand, before the great day arrived. They thanked the manager, and left.

On their way back to the Jeep, they were surprised to see Aengus striding toward them from the direction of the Whale Club.

He greeted them with his usual smile, but it was Sarah who seemed especially glad to see him. She may also have been the first to notice the fierceness that lay behind the kindness in his eyes.

Zoe had to admit that he was an unusual man. He was at ease with everyone, but didn't seem to fit anywhere, not even with those who worked at the Faire.

He appeared to be both young and old. Like someone from the past who was, somehow, lost in time.

Aengus asked Sarah if she had recovered from the incident with the would-be thief.

She grinned and assured him that both she and Woolf were fine.

"I've been touring the Whale Club," he explained, "and now I'm on my way to see the Lighthouse."

As he turned away, Sarah, who had been working up her courage, tugged at his sleeve and asked, "Would you mind if I drew a portrait of you, sometime?"

He looked at her questioningly for a moment, then threw back his head and laughed.

"Young Sarah, you're interested in more than just painting my portrait. But that's fine. You need to prove something to yourself, and there's no fault in that, girl."

Sarah was embarrassed and quickly looked down at her feet. But he gently touched her shoulder and she met his eyes, again.

"I'll be here when you're here, at this place, Sarah," he said. "You can draw me between waiting on customers. Okay?"

She nodded. "Thank you."

Once he was a distance away, Zoe asked, "What did he mean about your needing to prove something, Sarah?"

The girl shrugged. "I don't know, maybe I need to prove that I can draw a good portrait of him."

Zoe suspected there was more to it, but she let it go. Maybe his face held a particular kind of artistic challenge for Sarah.

Later that afternoon, it occurred to her to wonder how he knew that Sarah would be selling her things at the Lighthouse Gift Shop. Someone must have mentioned it. After all, the event was no secret.

Although they weren't due at the Faire for another hour, they decided to go early and eat lunch.

There was no shortage of choices and, in the end, Zoe opted for a "medieval" salad liberally sprinkled with edible flowers, while the girls chose huge, roasted turkey legs and potato salad.

By the time they finished, it was nearly 2:00 and time for Sarah and Kate to report to their tents.

Kate's was the closest, so they went there first and found Mandy already dressed in a deep-blue, velvet, gown with a sash that was a shade lighter, made of silk moire.

Zoe doubted whether the costume was authentic-looking, but it was definitely gorgeous and it suited Mandy, whose golden-brown hair was pulled up into a chignon, laced with pearls. She wore an ornate, pearl necklace and matching bracelet, as well.

Zoe jokingly wolf-whistled and Mandy dropped an exaggerated curtsey in their direction.

"Obviously," she gestured at the stalls behind her, "we've already mucked out here, and Bobby is getting the horses dressed up for our procession through the Faire."

Bobby was one of three teen-aged boys who were helping with the horses. His family owned a farm over on the mainland.

"Hopefully, I don't smell too much like a stable," Mandy remarked.

"Even if you did, no one would really care, would they? You look so gorgeous."

Mandy laughed. "Hey, love me—love my horses. I'll help Kate get into her things so you can get Sarah over to her art tent. We'll be riding out soon and we'll make a point of catching up with you over there."

As they turned to leave, another young man whom Mandy introduced as Ashton Phillips, rode up to join them. He was elegantly dressed as a Cavalier and he did look impressive, in spite of the white plume in his hat band that hung directly in his eyes.

"Give it here, Ashton, and let me see what I can do with it," Mandy grimaced.

Zoe wanted a photo of them, and decided to wait while Mandy quickly helped Kate into her dress.

"You take Woolf and go on ahead, Sarah. I'll hurry and catch up with you, shortly."

Once Kate was in her costume and Ashton's plume was sorted out, Zoe waited for them to mount-up. Unfortunately, just then, someone began to set off fireworks and Ashton's horse, Dancer, decided to live up to his name.

He grew more and more agitated and refused to allow Ashton to mount. Mandy quickly dismounted from her horse and ordered Kate to stay where she was.

She tightly gripped Dancer's bridle and tried to reassure him, but he was clearly having none of it.

Suddenly, an arm reached over Mandy's and took hold of the bridle. It was Aengus. Of course it would be, Zoe thought. The man seemed to turn up everywhere.

He quietly spoke into Dancer's ear and the horse stood still, quivering at first, then quickly becoming calm. Aengus slowly released the bridle and stood close, still stroking Dancer's head and murmuring some sort of "magic" words to him.

Mandy shook her head. "I've been around horses all my life, but that was remarkable. I've never seen one that upset, calm down so fast. What did you say to him?"

Aengus chuckled. "Actually, I gave him the words from a Gaelic lullaby. He seemed to like it as much as I did when I was a boy and my grandmother sang it to me." He turned to include all of them in his gaze.

"You know, animals are like people. You have to know how to talk to them, and above all, you have to respect them.

Don't fight them—respect them, instead. Try to see their point of view and you'll see a big difference in the way they respond to you."

Aengus's words seemed to have quieted the humans as much as they had the horse. It was as though he had cast a spell, and when he wished them a "good day" and left, no one spoke.

Once he was gone, each of them had the strange feeling that they had just been awakened from a very long and deep sleep.

Chapter 25

Late that afternoon, Hugh looked up as Jake walked into his office waving some papers.

"Just got these back on the Brents and thought you'd like to be the first to read them."

He thrust the papers across the desk. Hugh leaned forward to take them while Jake folded his arms and waited for a reaction.

Hugh carefully scanned the pages, then handed them back. "Nope," he shook his head. "There's nothing there."

"No police records, no outstanding warrants, not even a parking violation. Same thing on his wife."

Jake sat down in the chair opposite Hugh's desk and said, "That doesn't mean that one of them, or even both of them, didn't do it, Hugh. You know that. And so far, they're our best bet."

Hugh shrugged. "So what's next?" Jake asked him. "Harper and Jimmy didn't come back with anything new, either."

"I wish I knew." Hugh rubbed his eyes and his partner noticed the dark circles that hadn't been there before.

"It could have been anyone, I guess," he stifled a yawn. "We'll keep an eye on both houses as much as we can, but let's face it, I may have judged this completely wrong. Maybe Susan did just fall off that chair."

"Who else might we consider?" Jake persisted.

Without waiting for an answer, he said, "There's that Aengus person. Or that man who tried to rob Sarah could be a suspect. Let's face it, that one is definitely a nut-job."

"Yes, he is," Hugh agreed. "But this incident happened before the Faire arrived, so I seriously doubt that it was either of them. And besides, what would be their motive?"

Jake said, "We don't know anything about these men. For all we know, they might have been in the area before the Faire came."

"But if they had been, someone would have seen them, wouldn't they? Someone here would know something, which takes us back to the possibility that someone from here is trying to settle a grudge."

Hugh threw the papers down. "I still have this gut feeling that it isn't that simple. I don't know, maybe my gut is wrong. It probably wouldn't be the first time."

"Look," Jake hesitated, "This is none of my business, but you're exhausted, Hugh. It's a wonder you can think straight about anything, just now."

"Why don't you take a day off? Get away from here, go fishing or whatever you need to do to feel better."

Hugh's laugh was hollow. "I can't leave right now and you know that. Not until this damned Faire ends, anyway. Besides which, I have to get some other things straightened out pretty quickly, too."

Jake didn't ask what those 'things' were, but he had a pretty good idea. He'd seen Hugh with that woman called Maggie quite a lot recently, and that bothered him.

He'd known a few women like Maggie before, and they weren't the kind you wanted to stick with. Not for long, anyway.

"Okay," Hugh abruptly stood up. "Let's get over to the Faire. And meanwhile, go ask Jimmy to keep an eye on Susan's house today. We'll line up someone else to do it tonight."

144

"You can call me crazy, as long as you don't do it to my face," he joked, "but I can't let go of the feeling that something is wrong over there."

"Maybe it's not a vendetta. Maybe Susan just happened to get in the way of something else. We both know that empty houses can be used by smugglers, so maybe something like that is going on."

Jake nodded and went to find Jimmy while Hugh grabbed his car keys. He was relieved that Jake hadn't said anything more about Ivan. But he also knew that it was only a matter of time before he did.

If he could just get through this week without having to explain about Maggie and her brother to his partner, it would be a miracle. Then, they would be gone.

In his heart, he knew it wasn't that easy. There was a good chance the two of them wouldn't be leaving when the Faire did.

He was also well-aware that, for the time being, he was Maggie's prisoner and that included putting up with her repulsive brother, as well.

Would Zoe wait for him? He hoped so. He was going to have to talk to her again, very soon, and he debated if he should just tell her the truth.

She might leave him if he did, but then again, she might just leave him, anyway.

Chapter 26

The closer he got to Zoe's house, the more uneasy Hugh felt. On the way over, he had even rehearsed what he would say, but in his heart he felt that nothing he had come up with, so far, was good enough.

Whatever he said would probably be wrong anyway, and the entire future of their relationship could hinge on what happened this afternoon.

Thank heaven the Faire was nearly over with, not that its leaving would solve his problems.

By the time he reached her house, he was considering the possibility of leaving the area and finding a job elsewhere—preferably a long way away from the Outer Banks.

At the same time, just the thought of doing that made him feel unbearably empty.

As he pulled up, he saw that she wasn't home. He got out and stared at the house, debating whether he should stay or go.

Standing around and waiting was more than he could handle just then, so he decided to leave.

As he turned back to his car, he caught a glimpse of movement near the rippling waves opposite the house.

A man was standing on the shore, shielding his eyes with his hand and looking out over the sea. The dazzling sun on the water was enough to blind anyone.

Then, Hugh realized that the man was Aengus.

Aengus hadn't seen noticed Hugh. His focus was on the sea before him.

Somewhat reluctantly, Hugh decided that the right thing would be to speak to him. After all, he had helped Sarah when Ivan had bullied her.

He strolled toward the water and as he drew closer, Aengus spoke without turning to look at him.

"I've seen quite a few dolphins out here, today. You know they're magical creatures, don't you?" He sighed. "But then all creatures are magical in their own way, aren't they."

Hugh couldn't think of a good reply, so he stood next to Aengus and looked out at the sea, as well. Sure enough, a dolphin surfaced just then, leaped above the water and dove again. They really were amazing creatures.

"I've seen them from time to time, but I'm usually too busy to pay much attention. There are always a million things to do…." His voice faded into nothing.

"And no doubt to worry about, as well," Aengus replied in his lilting voice. Hugh gave him a quick look, but couldn't decide if he was being sarcastic or not.

Aengus knelt down and picked up a perfect little shell, a mollusk with raspberry striping. "Have you ever noticed how each of these is a miraculous work of art?" he asked. And each is a world unto itself, as well."

Hugh looked closely at the shell that lay in Aengus's hand as though he'd never seen one before. And perhaps he hadn't.

As if reading his thoughts, Aengus said, "Most people plunge through life without seeing what is around them. They seldom stop and really look, you know."

Hugh's gaze turned back to the sea and he wondered if the dolphin would surface.

"Feeling better?" Aengus asked.

"I'm fine," Hugh snapped, then apologized. "Sorry about that. Yeah, actually, I am. But how did you...?"

Aengus flashed his gentle smile. "It was written all over your face, but I could feel your tension, too."

Hugh stared at him. Aengus hadn't seen his face, to begin with. He bent over and picked up another perfect shell and handed it to Hugh.

"Here," he said. "Keep this with you and when you start to worry, take it out and look at it.

You will remember me, and it will also remind you to look around and let go of whatever worries you."

"I guess you'll be leaving soon," Hugh commented. "Where are you heading next?"

Aengus drew in a deep breath and exhaled. "A long way from here."

He looked up at the sky and watched a blue heron fly overhead, then glanced at Hugh.

"You'll have to settle this soon, you know. It won't keep until the Faire is gone, if that's what you're hoping for."

Hugh stared at him, again. "Who are you? What do you know about it, and why is it your business?"

"You're right," he said. "It's not my business, and you don't have to take my advice," he shrugged.

"That's entirely up to you. I'm just passing through and I know what I know. That's how it is." He glanced at the sun.

"I should get back to the Faire. I had tea with Susan earlier," he pointed in the direction of her house. "She'll be fine. It will all come together. See you later," he said.

He briefly rested a hand on Hugh's shoulder, then walked away. It wasn't until he was out of sight that Hugh realized that Aengus was walking. He surely had to have a vehicle somewhere hereabouts; it was much too far to walk back to the Renaissance Faire.

Just as Hugh opened his car door, Zoe pulled up next to the house.

The driver's door opened along with the others, and Hugh called out, "Hi, Girls, have you had a good day?"

He grinned at Kate and Sarah who looked at him uncertainly. Kate, always the bolder of the two, slowly returned his grin and said, "Yeah, it's been a good day."

Sarah looked at the ground instead of at him and to his surprise, Hugh felt hurt. He'd thought he had a good relationship with both girls.

But he also knew that once trust was lost, it was sometimes hard to find. And it was only natural that their loyalty would lay with their mother.

He stepped between the girls and grasped Zoe's elbow. "Can we walk?"

She gave him a questioning look, then turned to the girls and handed Kate her keys.

"Here Kate, you two go on in and get something to eat. I'll only be a minute."

Chapter 27

They walked a little distance from the house before Zoe abruptly pushed ahead and turned to face him.

"Okay, what did you want to say to me?" He could see that she was trying to look stern, but was only partially succeeding. That, at least, was good.

Hugh struggled to find the right words.

"You remember Zoe, that I asked you to trust me? That I couldn't tell you everything, but that you'd need to trust me?"

"Yes," she nodded. "So what's different now? Can you finally explain why you've been out of touch with me this week?"

"Well, the thing is," he hesitated, "I still can't really talk about it. But I do love you and I miss you, and so-help-me, I will resolve the problem and tell you all about it very soon."

"I've just been worried that you might give up on me before I had a chance to do that."

She folded her arms and looked down at the sand. "Tell me, do you have a plan as to the best way to resolve whatever you can't tell me about?"

"More or less," he admitted. "You just have to trust me. Can you do that for a few more days?"

She unfolded her arms and sighed. "How can you assume that I do or don't trust you when you haven't talked to me, since then?"

Hugh bent over to pick up a shell and thought about what Aengus had said earlier. He'd said not to wait until the Faire was over with to resolve things.

Maybe he was wrong. His advice was only his opinion, after all.

"Hugh?" Zoe brought him back to the present moment. "You were far away just then," she observed.

"Yeah, well…I'll tell you everything now rather than lose you. But if you can trust me a little longer, then I wouldn't be breaking my word to anyone." He looked at her hopefully.

"Whose secret are you keeping? Is it Maggie's? Because if so, then why would I care whether you kept your word to her or not, especially since I don't seem to mean as much to you as she does."

"She is playing an enormous game with you, Hugh. And you can do what you want, but I refuse to play it, too!" She turned and stalked back toward the house.

He debated whether to go after her, but decided against it. If she couldn't trust him a little longer, then maybe it was all for the best anyway. He would just leave the area like he'd been thinking of doing, anyway.

Zoe had abruptly turned away because tears welled up in her eyes and she didn't want Hugh to know. That was weakness, she told herself. And she couldn't afford to be weak.

She wondered if she should have agreed to trust him a little longer. She was sure that Maggie was playing some sort of a game.

Hugh was basically a good-hearted man, but he also was capable of being fooled into believing whatever 'secret' Maggie chose to feed him as truth.

Was their relationship over with? She wondered if this was the last she would see of him.

The girls were in the kitchen waiting, and she pasted a quick smile on her face in spite of still wanting to cry.

"Come on, grab your things if you're ready," she said, suddenly in a greater rush than she needed to be.

"Do we have to leave now, Mom? " Kate asked. "I thought we had a few more minutes before we have to go."

"You do, Kate; I'm just anxious to get over there. I think I'll go back to Susan's place while you and Sarah are busy."

"Let's see, I need a pad of paper and a pen, and they'll be upstairs. I'll be right back."

The girls exchanged looks but didn't say anything.

A few minutes later, Zoe reappeared with her briefcase. "Are you ready?"

"Yup," Sarah answered. "We had everything ready to go anyway."

She picked up the book bag that was filled with jewelry-making equipment as well as her watercolor paper and paints. Her costume was draped over her arm.

"Great, then let's get going. I don't know how long it will take me to go through those things at Susan's."

Chapter 28

Zoe didn't seem to notice that she was unusually quiet on the drive to the Renaissance Faire, but the girls did. To them, the drive seemed to take longer than usual, and they kept glancing nervously in the mirror at her, along the way.

"Is everything okay, Mom?" Kate finally ventured to ask. She leaned over to rest her head against Woolf's. Zoe glanced at her in the mirror and recognized the gesture as one that Kate had done since she was a little girl. It was a gesture of affection, but also one that told of her need for comfort.

"Katy, everything is up in the air with Hugh, just now. But that doesn't mean that it won't be okay. And meanwhile, you and I and Sarah are fine, and that's what matters most to me."

"Woolf, too," Kate grinned and raised her head to look at him. "Woolf is a very important part of our family, too, isn't he?"

Zoe grinned back at her in the mirror. "That goes without saying, as you very well know, Ms. Kate. Isn't that right, Ms. Sarah?"

Sarah lifted her head from the pages of the old mythology book she had been looking at. She seemed to carry it with her everywhere, these days. She grinned and made a thumbs-up sign.

Not long after, they pulled into the lane that ended at Susan's house. As they unloaded their things and locked the Jeep, Zoe glanced over at the Brent's place, and wondered if Noah or his wife had played any part in Susan's accident. She hadn't thought to ask Hugh what he'd found out.

When they reached the Faire, they saw a long line of people waiting to enter. Renee's fund-raiser had turned out very well, and Zoe wondered if they should bring the Faire back next year.

They went to find Mandy, first. She was already dressed in her blue, velvet gown and was ready to ride.

Kate ran to her and they both waved at Zoe and Sarah before disappearing inside the tent where Kate would change.

Her costume was a rose-colored, velvet gown that made Zoe realize, more than she wanted to, that Kate was not a little girl, anymore.

Her long, light-brown hair was pulled back with invisible clips, and she wore a wreath of tiny, matching-pink roses. Her blue eyes seemed to shine brighter whenever she wore her costume.

Their next stop was the art tent, where a small section had been screened off for students who needed privacy to change into their costumes.

Sarah quickly stepped behind the screen and Zoe helped her put on the emerald-green satin dress that perfectly suited her dark hair and eyes.

Like Kate's, her hair was clipped back and she wore a wreath of light-pink roses with green ribbons, and looked much too grown up.

Afterward, Zoe went to see if Renee was free to go with her to Susan's house. But she wasn't in her garden-shed office, so Zoe went to buy herself a drink, instead.

But then she glanced at her watch and decided to go on to Susan's, so that she could get back in time to see the jousting. That particular event always drew large crowds, and she especially enjoyed it.

She avoided the area where Maggie's tent was, in case Hugh was there. But as she was leaving, Maggie quickly brushed past her and then turned and gave her a brilliant smile before proceeding on her way.

Zoe shivered. That strange smile felt like a threat. Or, was it a smile of victory?

She hurried toward Susan's house wondering about the secret that Maggie had sworn Hugh to keep.

Whatever it was, made her angry all over again. There was nothing to do except wait and see what happened.

If Hugh would only confide in her, she might be able to help him see what was really going on behind Maggie's words.

Chapter 29

The house was stuffy when Zoe entered, and she wondered how it managed to feel both stuffy and chilly at the same time.

She didn't intend to stay long, especially since she was on her own, but she did need to at least make more progress and the girls knew where she was in case anything happened.

Nearly an hour later, Zoe had managed to get through most of what Susan and Rose had piled on the dining room table.

Looking around, she decided to take a quick look in the corner cupboard just in case they had missed anything interesting.

She opened the bottom door and saw something silver stuck way in the back. The cupboard was so deep that she had to half-crawl inside it to reach whatever was there. It was no wonder they had overlooked it.

She carefully backed out again, holding tightly to an old, coin-silver spoon. She thought it might be English. She straightened up, but before she could examine the mark, there was a footstep and someone grabbed her from behind.

A sickly-smelling cloth was tightly pressed to her nose and she quickly lost her ability to fight. She couldn't breathe. Then everything went dark.

When Zoe finally awoke, the sky was dark and she could see the glimmer of early stars through a nearby window.

Her hands and legs were bound and something, perhaps a scarf, was stuffed in her mouth. She was on the floor, leaning against a bed.

Her head pounded. Had her attacker hit her in the head? She didn't think so, but she couldn't be sure. He had to have either dragged or carried her upstairs; maybe he'd banged her head on something, in the process.

She looked closer and though the room was dark, she thought she must be in Susan's old bedroom.

It was hard to tell and it probably didn't matter, anyway. It wasn't like she could get up and run away. She began to panic. Kate and Sarah were the only ones who knew where she was, and hopefully, by now, they had already gone for help.

Heavy footsteps slowly climbed the stairs. Whoever it was, certainly made no attempt to be quiet. She held her breath and waited.

Sure enough, she heard the creak of the bedroom door and then a flashlight suddenly shone directly into her face.

A large man grunted as he squatted on his heels to look at her. To her horror, it was Ivan, the man who had bullied Sarah.

"Okay, Lady," he giggled as he sat down opposite so he could better see her face.

"Not so high and mighty without your deputy here to protect you, are you? Let me explain, that's because he's with my sister and she's keeping him busy for me."

"Hell, she's been keeping him busy all week!" he cackled, then put his face closer to hers.

He was drunk; she could smell liquor on his breath. He was also taunting her, and in spite of her fear, she was determined not to give him the satisfaction of knowing that his words stung her.

"You didn't know that, did you?" he asked, as he closely watched her.

"You thought he was your fella, but he's not. Yeah, I know all about you and Hugh. In fact, I know *all* the local gossip that's worth knowing around this place."

He leaned over and roughly pulled the cloth out of her mouth.

"I'm doing this because there is no point in your screaming for help. No one can hear you. But if you decide to try it anyway, I will break your skull with my bare hands. You got that?"

Zoe nodded. Small pieces of lint stuck to her mouth and she licked her lips. "Who are you?" she asked. "And how do you know anything about the local gossip?"

If she was going to die anyway, she might as well ask. Besides which, if she kept him talking, someone might turn up to rescue her.

He sat back on his heels. "Since we're going to be spending the next hour or so together before I kill you, I guess it won't hurt to say what's what," he gloated, his small eyes sparkling with glee.

"Your deputy's new girlfriend is my sister. You know, Maggie? Pretty little Maggie. Prettier than you are, that's for sure," he chortled.

"As for how I know the gossip, that's down to Noah Brent. See, he's my cousin. Our cousin," he corrected himself. "Mine and Maggie's."

"So, he's in on this?" her voice quavered in spite of her attempt to show no fear. "Does he know what you're doing here?"

"Nah" he shook his head. "He didn't want nothing to do with my plans. But we're family, see? So he ain't gonna rat me out to nobody either."

"Are you sure about that?" Zoe shot back.

Ivan ignored her and pulled out his cell phone. He looked at it for a moment then stuffed it back into his pocket.

"It's time to go, and you've probably guessed that you're going with me, right? You're my ticket out of this, if any problems come up."

He glanced around at the room. "I'm gonna burn this place, and at first, I was gonna burn you with it."

"But then I got to thinking that you'd make a great hostage. At least until we're clear of here, then I'll get rid of you."

"Does your sister know about this?" Zoe asked.

"She knows enough," he admitted, "but she don't care what I do as long as we stick together. And besides, she don't have no use for the Wellford family, either."

Zoe's desperation was growing. "What did Susan do to deserve this? Did you push her off that chair, too? How did you get into the house?"

He laughed. "Whoa! That's a lot of questions, but we have a few minutes and it won't matter how much I tell you, now." He was obviously proud of himself and eager to brag about what he'd done.

"It wasn't hard to get a key to this place. Noah had one from years ago, and nobody's bothered to change the locks since then."

He frowned. "At first, he didn't want to give it to me. But I told him that if he didn't, he and his crazy wife would live to regret it. So he gave it to me like I knew he would. He was always weak. Scared of his own shadow, old Noah is."

"But why attack Susan?" she persisted. "It's not like she did anything to you, and she's not responsible for whatever her family might have done years ago."

162

"Oh, it's nothing personal," he waved his hand dismissively. "She's just one of them and that's all that matters."

He reached over to pick up a small gas can and maliciously grinned at her. With some effort, he dragged himself to his feet and liberally sprinkled the liquid around the room before he looked at her, again.

"It's gasoline," he explained. "I was gonna use kerosene, but I found out that gas burns better. Maybe you didn't know that, but you soon will." His high-pitched giggle echoed off the walls.

"I'll start the fire here, and that'll give me time to get us out before the downstairs catches, which shouldn't take too long."

He went into the hall and sprinkled more liquid on the bare floor-boards, then came back into the bedroom and sat the can down beside the bed.

"What did her family do to yours?" Zoe's voice was hoarse.

He drew himself up straight and put a large hand on either hip. He really was a big man, she thought. She had no doubt that he was strong enough to easily kill her with his bare hands.

"Susan Hill's grandad swindled my great-grandad out of a lot of money. In fact, if it wasn't for him," his huge hands tightened into fists, "then we'd be fine. We'd have plenty of money and we wouldn't be dragging around the East Coast with these stupid Renaissance Faires and festivals."

Zoe stifled the urge to point out that both he and his sister could have just settled down somewhere and found jobs, like most other people did.

It was clear that whatever he had in mind to do with her wasn't going to be good.

She thought of Kate and Sarah, and Woolf. What would happen to them if she wasn't around? Somehow, she had to get herself out of this mess.

At the moment though, nothing was coming to mind, and she could only hope that an opportunity would present itself along the way.

Ivan bent and easily lifted her from the floor. He threw her over his shoulder and carried her downstairs where he paused and looked around.

"It's a shame I couldn't have got more of this stuff out of here to sell," he said. "But that's the way it is. I can't wait any longer."

He laid her, none-too-gently, on the floor in the hall. "Now you stay put!" He wagged a playful finger at her and laughed at his own joke.

"I'm going to light this place up and then I'll be right back for you."

"Aren't you going to at least cut the rope around my legs?" she pleaded.

"You can't carry me all the way to your cousin's house or wherever we're going, without slowing yourself down."

He looked thoughtful. "Okay, I see your point. So in the meantime, I'll have to tie you to this stair railing."

He proceeded to cut the ropes that bound her legs and, with relief, she felt the blood starting to flow back into them.
At least if an opportunity arose, she might be able to run.

But her relief quickly ended when he painfully bound her hands to the railing. She knew that she couldn't stand the pain for very long, and wondered if she should take a chance and scream, after all.

Ivan was likely right about there being no one to hear her though, and she had to hang on in case there was an opportunity to get away from him.

Tears began to course down her face. She was terrified and the pain was unbearable. She wondered if she was really going to die, that night.

Just then, something crashed against the front door. Her already-shattered nerves made her cry out.

Two more crashes followed, and the door burst open. In came Woolf, who tore up the stairs, presumably after Ivan. Thankfully, he was closely followed by Aengus, then Hugh and the girls. Susan, who had just arrived in her car, ran in behind them.

Aengus's pocket-knife flashed and in an instant, Zoe was free. He said nothing, but charged up the stairs just as Hugh bellowed, "Stay here!" to the rest of them.

Hugh ran back out the front door, but he might as well have saved his breath because they all took off running after him.

Fortunately, Ivan hadn't had time to start a fire before he'd heard the front door give way.

Instead, he panicked and threw himself out the bedroom window. Aengus saw him disappear out the window, and ran back down the stairs to follow the others.

****

The howling wind contorted the trees, and the rising waves pounded the shore so that he couldn't hear the approaching hoof beats that thundered after him.

But perhaps it was the pounding of Ivan's own heart that deafened him most as he stumbled over the uneven ground, running for all he was worth.

He had jumped out the upstairs window so quickly that he had fallen down the ladder and had badly hurt his shoulder. He thought it might be broken.

It would only be moments before that German shepherd bolted back down the stairs and came after him. He couldn't outrun the dog, he knew that. But maybe he had enough of a head start to make it to shelter, anyway.

His breathing quickly turned to sobs as he ran. With every ounce of his strength, he heaved himself toward the safety of his cousin's house. Noah didn't approve of him, but after all, he was family.

Surely Noah would let him stay, even for half an hour, until he could safely get back to Maggie who would certainly protect him.

He suddenly became aware of another sound, and whatever it was, was gaining on him.

It sounded like the pounding hooves of a running horse, but he knew it couldn't be because the wild horses never came this far up the Sound. Maybe it was just the wind playing tricks on his mind.

He involuntarily turned his head and glanced to the right, where the sound was coming from, and saw a white horse galloping straight at him.

Moments later, Woolf cautiously approached the man where he lay, completely still. The dog threw his head back and produced a terrible, unearthly howl.

Hugh was the first to arrive, and he found Ivan with his mouth still open in a silent scream. His eyes were wide with fear.

By the light of the full moon, he saw the clear shape of the hoof print that had dented the man's skull on the right side, where blood still oozed from the wound.

Ivan had died from a powerful blow given by a horse. Hugh involuntarily shivered. He had a pretty good idea which horse it was, too.

Before he had time to take in what that meant, he saw the others running across the field toward him.

He quickly took off his jacket and threw it over the dead man's face. And as he did so, he looked up and saw a white horse standing quietly, a little distance away by the shore, his mane and tail whipped by the wind.

In spite of the distance, Hugh could see his blazing eyes. The others, who abruptly stopped next to him, saw it, as well.

"It's the Ghost Horse!" Kate cried out, as a sob caught in her throat.

The horse waited to make sure they saw him before he slowly faded and was absorbed into the evening mist.

Chapter 30

The rest of the evening was a blur when Zoe tried to recall everything that happened, later.

Once she and the others had caught up with Hugh and Woolf in the field, they had stood huddled together for comfort in the dark, keeping a distance between themselves and Ivan's body.

The only sounds were those of the wild wind and the waves.

As other officers arrived, Hugh laid his hand on Zoe's shoulder and told the small group to go back to the house.

He said, "They'll want to move the body soon, and you shouldn't be here."

His hand tightened on her shoulder as she began to turn away. "Zoe, I'm going to call an ambulance. You need to be checked out to make sure you're okay."

To her relief, she saw the old tenderness that had been there before Maggie came.

She shook her head. "I'm not going anywhere except home, Hugh. As soon as possible."

"Are you sure?" he gently grasped both her shoulders. "It would be best if a doctor saw you, tonight."

"No," she was adamant. "I am badly bruised, but that's all."

"Besides, I was able to run across this field with the rest of you, so obviously the effects of the ether have worn off too, and I'm okay."

"That could have just been your adrenalin kicking in," he smiled. "But if you think you're okay, then we'll let it go."

"I'll tell you what," he said, "wait for me at Susan's house and get her to make you something hot to drink. I'll send a couple of officers to take your statements very soon."

He turned away and the small group slowly walked back together. The wind felt good to Zoe. Or maybe it was just the knowledge that she wasn't going to die that night, after all.

She and the girls kept their arms around each other, and no one felt like talking.

When they reached the house, Zoe's eyes immediately went to the ropes that were still lying on the floor, and she shivered.

Susan scurried in behind them and pushed her way through to the kitchen where she filled a kettle with water to make tea. Zoe and the girls wearily followed, and took their places at the kitchen table.

"I was hoping you would find me before it was too late," Zoe said. "Tell me what happened."

Sarah was the first to speak. "You didn't come back when you should have, so I went to look for you, and I saw Kate looking for you, too."

"We were getting really scared and didn't know what to do. But then we saw Hugh. He asked where you had gone and we told him, and we all took off running as fast as we could."

"Somewhere along the way," she added, "Aengus caught up with us. But he out-ran us, so he got here first."

"He and Woolf, that is," she corrected herself.

Tears of relief flooded Zoe's eyes and the girls went to hug her just as Susan sat the teapot on the table in front of them.

"You all like cream and sugar, don't you?" she asked as she poured out mugs of steaming, strong tea and added more sugar than any of them preferred.

She pushed the mugs across to them and said, "Now you get that down and you'll feel better in no time."

"I mean it," she wagged her finger at them. "Drink it now while it's good and hot."

Zoe was surprised to see that her hands shook as she carefully lifted the mug and took a sip.

Two officers arrived just then to take their statements. They spent nearly an hour explaining and repeating what had happened, and just as they were wrapping up, Hugh walked into the kitchen.

"Are you finished?" He glanced at his watch.

"For now," one of the officers replied, looking over his notes. "And if we aren't, we'll come and find you tomorrow."

He grinned at them. "You all get some rest, and sleep well."

Hugh waited until they'd left, then looked around at each of them.

"Okay, I want to update you on what's going on," he said, suddenly realizing how dear they all were to him.

"Why don't you sit down first, Hugh," Susan said as she stifled a yawn.

He nodded and pulled out a chair. "Noah and his wife, and Maggie, are all on their way to the station for questioning."

"We need to determine how much they knew and whether or not they helped Ivan with his plans."

"It is possible," he added, "that they didn't know how far he'd gone with this, but we need to find out. The corker is that they are all related to each other."

"Ivan told me that," Zoe informed him. "And from what he said, they did at least know some of what was going on"

"He also told me that Noah actually had a key to this house and Ivan threatened him in order to get his own hands on it."

"It also sounded like Maggie was well-aware of his vendetta against Susan, but didn't try to discourage him."

"Maybe she didn't know that he going to take me as a hostage and then kill me." Zoe sat up straighter. "She couldn't have, because only the girls knew I was here."

"Unless one of them overheard you talking to the girls, and then he followed you here. That's always possible," Hugh said.

"Hopefully, she'll tell the truth," he added, "but I wouldn't count on it."

"She's a good actress and my guess is that she'll find a way to wiggle out of any part of this."

Zoe stared at him. "What do you mean she's a 'good actress'?"

"I'll explain later," he said. "Let me finish what I came to say, first."

"From what I could gather, someone in Susan's family had cheated Ivan's family out of a lot of money. Now, I can understand the anger and resentment, but the fact that it happened so many years ago is what makes this whole vendetta so preposterous to me."

"Why now? I mean, what triggered the attacks after all this time, when he could have done these things any time?"

"Maybe his grudge kept growing over the years, "Zoe speculated. "Maybe it grew stronger and stronger over time because he continued to brood on it."

"But, we also have to remember that he was a bully, and bullies need victims. Maybe that tendency grew, as well. I can't pretend that I'm sorry he's gone," she added.

"I'm pretty sure that only Maggie will miss him," Hugh sighed. "It's pretty sad."

"The sins of the fathers…" Susan muttered.

"No." Zoe stopped her. "This has nothing to do with you, Susan. What happened here was no judgement against you from a Higher Power. This was only an evil plot concocted by an evil man."

"Pretty much," Hugh agreed with her. "Finish up your tea everybody. I'm going to take you home and you can pick up your vehicles tomorrow. You too, Susan."

Zoe and Susan both insisted that they would drive themselves, so he reluctantly gave in.

"Okay…but I'm going to follow you to make sure you get home safe," he told them. Zoe opened her mouth.

"I don't want any argument from you, about it," he sternly said, then flashed a grin at her.

"By the way," he looked around. "Where is Aengus?" They all looked at each other.

"I don't know," Susan answered. "I think he walked back with us, but he didn't come into the house, did he?"

"No, he didn't," the others agreed. It was odd that none of them had missed him sooner.

"I suppose he's just gone back to the Faire." Hugh yawned and stretched his arms. "I'll need to catch up with him later tonight. But first, I want to get you all home."

Zoe and Susan lived near each other, and as soon as Susan parked beside her house and got out, she turned to wave.

"Do you want to come in for a while?" Zoe called to her. "I'm still too keyed up to sleep and maybe you are, too."

"No, thanks," she called back. "I am so tired that I just want to go to bed. I'll come by in the morning for coffee, instead."

She really was too tired. Now that it was all over with, her knees felt weaker than she wanted to admit to anyone.

She firmly closed her door as Kate and Sarah slowly walked around to the back of their own house.

Sarah stumbled over a clump of grass growing in the sand, but caught herself just as her sister reached out to help.

"Good-night," they waved, as Kate fished in her bag for the house key.

Once they were safely inside, Hugh reached for Zoe and turned her to face him. "We need to talk, Honey, and I promise that I'm going to tell you everything."

"As a matter of fact," he explained, "I was already looking for you at the Faire when the girls found me, because no matter what, I don't want to lose you. I don't want to keep any secrets from you, either."

Zoe leaned against him and his arms came round her as she snuggled close.

"I'm so relieved, Hugh. And I want to hear it all, every bit of it. Do you want to come in now and talk?"

"I would," he reluctantly answered, "but I need to find Aengus and get back to the station."

"Tomorrow is the last day of the Faire, and Sarah's event at the Lighthouse. Let's get past all that and then tomorrow night I'll tell you everything you want to know. And probably more besides," he chuckled.

Chapter 31

The next golden afternoon found Hugh with Zoe and Kate, watching the activity at the Renaissance Faire where vendors were already beginning to pack up.

There were still plenty of customers scurrying around to do last-minute shopping for the hand-crafted items they wanted, and a couple more shows were still scheduled.

By later that night, almost everyone would leave and by late the next morning, the Faire would only be a memory.

A clean-up crew was scheduled to arrive bright and early to remove whatever litter was left in the field.

Some of the vendors were shouting early good-byes to one another, but they were an altogether more subdued group than they had been when they'd arrived.

Zoe thought it was probably due to Ivan's death and Maggie's possible involvement.

She had been released for the time being, because Hugh said there hadn't been enough evidence to arrest her. She had also been sternly warned to remain in the area until the police told her she could leave.

Noah and Annalee had been released, as well. The police had seen, first-hand, that they had both been tortured by Ivan.

Noah's wrists were raw from being tied, and he had a black eye and some bad bruising on the side of his face.

Analee's face was also bruised, and one of her front teeth was missing; the result of being punched in the mouth by a large fist.

It was obvious, Hugh said, that neither had willingly consented to help him.

Maggie's story, he explained, didn't entirely make sense, and so she was still a 'person of interest.'

Hugh believed that she would try to run away, and half-hoped that she would. An officer had been assigned to watch her, and he wondered if she was aware of that.

Kate reluctantly waved good-by to the Renaissance Faire as they headed back to Zoe's Jeep. It was parked at Susan's house were roofers were already at work, outside. Inside, electricians were busy completely rewiring the house.

Susan was more at peace than she had been for a very long time. She smiled broadly when she saw them coming, and ran outside to offer them coffee from a carafe that she'd brought from her home.

"I'm going to get these old rooms painted as soon as the rest of it is in good, working order," she told them.

"This has been a creepy, old house, but I'm going to make it as pleasant and happy as possible. Getting all of the old things out should help, too."

They followed her inside. "Have you decided what to do with it?" Zoe looked around at the piles of things that had been sorted to go to various places.

Some of it would be donated and some would be sold. The really good pieces were being purchased by an antique dealer whom Zoe knew in Virginia, and Susan had already removed everything she wanted to keep, to her own house.

"I'm going to rent it for the time being," she said with satisfaction. "I may eventually sell it, but for now, I can't quite bring myself to part with it."

She laughed at herself. "And to think that for all these years, I couldn't wait to get rid of it. What a difference a day makes. Or several days in this case."

"Maybe it isn't really haunted, after all," Zoe remarked as she drifted through the downstairs rooms. "Maybe what we felt was simply the unhappiness of the house, itself."

"That's why I think painting and getting rid of these things will help," Susan nodded.

"Some people say that houses, and land, and sometimes even the things we own, hold memory."

"However," she added, "the house definitely is haunted."

Zoe looked at her and smiled. "Somehow, that does not surprise me,"

Hugh threw back his head and laughed, then gently tugged on a strand of Kate's hair. "What do you think, Ms. Kate?"

She nodded as she looked around the room they were standing in. "I'm not surprised either," she said. "I've thought there were ghosts here, but what's happened to make you so sure?"

Susan smiled. "One of the electricians had to go to the attic, which has its own stair-case."

She looked at Zoe. "Do you remember my telling you that I hadn't been up there in years, and didn't want to go near it again until I had to?"

Zoe nodded, "Yes, I do."

"Well," Susan continued, "he was working up there, and at one point, he straightened up and turned around to grab a tool."

"That's when he saw an old man leaning on two canes. The man was standing close to him, glaring at him."

"Evidently, the electrician threw down his tools and ran for the stairs. And I was told that he has refused to go back up there alone."

"So now," she added, they will only go to the second floor and to the attic in pairs, because no one will go alone."

"The old devil—though it's hard to say just which 'old devil' it is—knowing my family," she giggled, "has taken up residence there."

"I'll tell you what though," she added, "before I rent this house, I'm going to find a priest to come and 'lay' him to rest along with anyone else who might be lingering here."

Chapter 32

Aengus was nowhere to be found. Hugh thought he would surely show up at the Currituck Lighthouse that afternoon because Aengus had promised to let Sarah draw him. Hugh asked Sarah to tell him to get in touch before he left the area.

When Hugh, Zoe, and Kate drove over to the Lighthouse to pick up Sarah, they found her in a good mood. She had sold quite a lot of jewelry, and a few paintings, and had enjoyed herself.

"Did Aengus come by?" Hugh asked as he gazed around at the crowd of departing guests.

"No," she shook her head as she packed up her things. "But it's okay. I didn't really expect him to, after what happened the other night."

"What do you mean, Sarah?" Zoe asked. "What possible difference could Ivan's death have made to him?"

"He wasn't related too, was he?" She gave Hugh a questioning look.

"I think it was everything that happened," Sarah said. "You know, so much violence and hatred for no good reason."

"Things like that bother him. And besides, he's on a quest."

"A quest? Did he tell you that?" Zoe's eyebrows rose.

"Not in so many words," Sarah answered. "But he's searching and will keep searching, and," she met their eyes, "I also think he was here to help."

Zoe and Hugh exchanged looks. "Do you mean with the Faire, or the situation with Ivan and Susan?" Zoe asked.

"I don't know for sure," she admitted. "Maybe both. But think about it. He helped all of us, in his own way."

"That's certainly true, Honey," Zoe agreed. She looked at Hugh again, and he nodded.

"You have a lot of good intuition, Sarah, and I think you're right about him. I'm sorry you didn't get to draw him, though."

Sarah shrugged. "Honestly, it really doesn't matter." That seemed strange to Zoe but she decided to let it go.

Later that evening when the stars had begun to show themselves, Zoe and Hugh walked along the shore holding hands.

The girls were watching a movie and Woolf had been left behind, as well.

Being together again was a relief for them both—like waking from a nightmare that neither had perhaps fully understood.

The moon was growing brighter when Hugh stepped in front of her and took her hands. "And now, it is time to talk and I am going to tell you everything."

She smiled at his serious expression. "I'm ready whenever you are."

"Good." He looked out at the sea and then back at her and cleared his throat.

"I knew Maggie some years back, as you already know. She was beautiful and bewitching, and I fell in love with her, or at least I thought I had."

"But the truth is, the longer I was with her, the more alarmed I became. She was always a little unstable, but eventually I came to see that something was seriously wrong with her."

"I should have broken off with her then," he tightened his hold on Zoe's hands, "but she was so fragile, and it seemed easier and best for everyone if I just unofficially faded out of her life."

"It seemed to work fine—as you know, I didn't see or hear any more from her."

"Well, I do envy her in a way," Zoe said, and Hugh looked at her in surprise.

"I seriously doubt that anyone will ever describe me as 'beautiful and bewitching. But Maggie really is lovely and I can see why you were attracted to her."

"Yeah, but that's the thing," he explained. "I didn't stay attracted very long. And in the end, I could hardly bear to even look at her, much less be around her."

"You see, it didn't take long for me to realize that her beauty is only an illusion—it's not real. She's not real. Whereas," he went on, "your beauty is real, and solid, and sane."

"Okay," she mock-sighed. "I guess I'll have to settle for unromantic words like 'solid and sane,' then."

He sheepishly grinned. "That's not quite what I meant, and you know it."

She shrugged. "Maybe. Go on."

"Well," he continued, "when I saw her again, she told me that she'd had a breakdown after we parted. She also thought it was a miracle that had brought *us* back together again, too."

Zoe half-tried to stifle an impatient snort. "Oh, please. I hardly think so, unless she was referring to some kind of demonic intervention that brought you together."

Hugh laughed. "Maggie asked me not to tell anyone about her breakdown because her friends didn't know…"

"So you're telling me that she actually has friends?" Zoe asked.

Hugh laughed again. "Will you stop it?" He leaned over and kissed her forehead.

"I'm trying to explain all this and you're not helping."

"Okay," she agreed, "I'll try. It's just such a dramatic, cock-and-bull story that I'm having trouble believing any of this is real."

"And it may not be," he agreed. "I'm just trying to explain what happened, if you'll let me do that."

"Anyway, she said that she still wanted people to respect her and you know how funny some people can be about a thing like that."

"Then," he paused and chose his words, "she told me that because fate had brought us together again, she would kill herself if I ever left her. She wanted to stay here and marry me."

"So what about Ivan? Would you have inherited him, too?" Zoe asked.

"Probably," he agreed. "The thing is, I was afraid that she really would kill herself, and I didn't know what to do."

"So I just foolishly hoped that by the end of the week, everything would have just sorted itself out, somehow."

Zoe pulled her hands away. "You are much too trusting, Hugh."

"That woman loves herself way-too-much to ever take her own life. I knew she was playing a game with you, all along." Her anger flared and she looked away.

"Yeah, well, I guess you were right," he said. "I was raised to keep a promise. But when I saw Aengus out here, he told me that whatever needed to be resolved wouldn't wait until the Faire was over with, and now I see that he was right."

He sighed. "If I had told you about this sooner, we might have worked out a good way to handle it—handle her, I mean."

She was still looking away from him and at the sea when he took her hands again and lifted them to his lips. "I am so very sorry, Zoe. I love you and I want to marry you more than anything in this world. But can you ever forgive me and trust me?"

Zoe looked into his eyes. "Yes, though I will admit that I did wonder if I could. But I know that deep-down it was your own good nature and her evil one that created this problem."

"And I know for sure that you were not deliberately trying to deceive me."

"I'm not sure that Maggie is really evil..." he began, and she interrupted him.

"Excuse me, but yes she is because she deliberately manipulated you against your will in order to get what she wanted. That qualifies as 'evil' in my book."

"Just let her go, Zoe. I already have, and we need to focus on us, instead. Will you marry me?"

He dramatically sank down on one knee and she laughed. "Honestly, Hugh, get up off that wet sand. First, I need to know if you have completely and officially broken up with Maggie."

He smiled. "Yes, I did. In fact, I broke up with her before setting out to look for you at the Faire when the girls found me."

"You weren't afraid anymore that she would kill herself?" Zoe asked.

"By that time, I had recognized that I was her hostage, and that I was not responsible for either her life or her death."

"It was past time for me to just be honest with her and then walk away. So I did."

"How did she take that?" There was a sense of awe in Zoe's voice.

"Not well, as you can imagine. She screamed and cried, and threw a basket of flowers at me. And I left."

"And now," he sank back down on one knee, "will you please marry me?"

She shook her head at him and grinned "Please get up."

He obeyed, and then took her in his arms and kissed her. When they broke apart, she whispered, "Yes, I'll marry you."

They returned to the house soon after to find the girls sitting on the couch, looking at Sarah's old mythology book.

"Are you ever going to take that back to the library, Sarah?" Zoe asked. "You've had it for weeks now."

"Yes, but not right away. I got an extension on the due-date, again," she explained, then looked up at their smiling faces and nudged Kate, who also looked up and grinned.

"You guys are going to get married, aren't you?" Sarah asked.

They all burst out laughing at her blunt question. "Yes, we are," Hugh emphatically answered.

"That is, if it's okay with you girls."

"Are you kidding?" Kate shouted and threw her arms around her mother first, then him.

Zoe reached out for Sarah and they all hugged and clung to each other a moment before finally breaking apart once again.

"When?" Sarah asked with a huge grin on her face.

"We think this coming December." Zoe looked at Hugh and his eyes shone as he nodded his agreement.

"And now," her voice became brisk again, "how about some hot chocolate? I'll have it together in a jiffy."

"And Sarah, I am sorry that Aengus didn't come to have his picture drawn. It still doesn't seem like him to not follow through on a promise."

"I know," Hugh chimed in. "It was really odd when I went back to the Renaissance Faire to find him, because no one there knew who he was."

"They remembered him, but they thought he was a local person who was just interested in helping out. And all the time, *we* thought he was traveling with them!"

"Mom," Sarah said, "I have a confession to make. I didn't need to sketch Aengus in order to remember him."

"He was just so special, and I was drawn to him from the first time I saw him."

"But memories fade over time, Sarah," Zoe gently smoothed the girl's hair. "Maybe you should draw him now, while you clearly remember him."

"No," she shook her head. "And this is what I'm really confessing. I don't need to, because I already have a wonderful picture of him to copy."

Zoe and Hugh gave her a puzzled look as she passed her mythology book to them and pointed to one of the pages.

Kate got up to look too, and gasped as her mother cried out, "I can't believe it!"

Hugh grabbed the book and saw for himself that there, among the other beautiful illustrations of mythological gods and goddesses, was an exact likeness of Aengus. And the caption read,

"*Aengus, a Celtic god of love and youth whose search for a maiden he met in a dream, led him to travel long and far. When he finally found her, she had taken the form of a swan and was living as a member of a game of 150 swans.*

His task then, was to identify which of the swans was the woman he loved.

Jayne Conrad Harding lives in Virginia with her husband and three cats. In addition to writing, she enjoys travel, cooking, and being outdoors as much as possible, Jayne also teaches university classes in journalism writing, textual analysis, and composition.

Made in the USA
Middletown, DE
23 May 2021